THE SHADOW PEOPLE

Borgo Press Books by JOHN RUSSELL FEARN

1,000-Year Voyage: A Science Fiction Novel * *Anjani the Mighty: A Lost Race Novel* (Anjani #2) * *Black Maria, M.A.: A Classic Crime Novel* (Black Maria #1) * *A Case for Brutus Lloyd* * *The Crimson Rambler: A Crime Novel* * *Death in Silhouette* (Black Maria #5) * *Don't Touch Me: A Crime Novel* * *Dynasty of the Small: Classic Science Fiction Stories* * *The Empty Coffins: A Mystery of Horror* * *The Fourth Door: A Mystery Novel* * *From Afar: A Science Fiction Mystery* * *Fugitive of Time: A Classic Science Fiction Novel* * *The G-Bomb: A Science Fiction Novel* * *The Genial Dinosaur* (Herbert the Dinosaur #2) * *The Gold of Akada: A Jungle Adventure Novel* (Anjani #1) * *Here and Now: A Science Fiction Novel* * *Into the Unknown: A Science Fiction Tale* * *Last Conflict: Classic Science Fiction Stories* * *Legacy from Sirius: A Classic Science Fiction Novel* * *The Man from Hell: Classic Science Fiction Stories* * *The Man Who Was Not: A Crime Novel* * *Manton's World: A Classic Science Fiction Novel* * *Moon Magic: A Novel of Romance* (as Elizabeth Rutland) * *The Murdered Schoolgirl: A Classic Crime Novel* (Black Maria #2) * *One Remained Seated: A Classic Crime Novel* (Black Maria #3) * *One Way Out: A Crime Novel* (with Philip Harbottle) * *Pattern of Murder: A Classic Crime Novel* * *Reflected Glory: A Dr. Castle Classic Crime Novel* * *Robbery Without Violence: Two Science Fiction Crime Stories* * *Rule of the Brains: Classic Science Fiction Stories* * *Shattering Glass: A Crime Novel* * *The Silvered Cage: A Scientific Murder Mystery* * *Slaves of Ijax: A Science Fiction Novel* * *Something from Mercury: Classic Science Fiction Stories* * *The Space Warp: A Science Fiction Novel* * *A Thing of the Past* (Herbert the Dinosaur #1) * *Thy Arm Alone: A Classic Crime Novel* (Black Maria #4) * *The Time Trap: A Science Fiction Novel* * *Vision Sinister: A Scientific Detective Thriller* * *Voice of the Conqueror: A Classic Science Fiction Novel* * *What Happened to Hammond? A Scientific Mystery* * *Within That Room!: A Classic Crime Novel* * *World Without Chance*

THE GOLDEN AMAZON SAGA

1. *World Beneath Ice* * 2. *Lord of Atlantis* * 3. *Triangle of Power* * 4. *The Amethyst City* * 5. *Daughter of the Amazon* * 6. *Quorne Returns* * 7. *The Central Intelligence* * 8. *The Cosmic Crusaders* * 9. *Parasite Planet* * 10. *World Out of Step* * 11. *The Shadow People* * 12. *Kingpin Planet* * 13. *World in Reverse* * 14. *Dwellers in Darkness* * 15. *World in Duplicate* * 16. *Lords of Creation* * 17. *Duel with Colossus* * 18. *Standstill Planet* * 19. *Ghost World* * 20. *Earth Divided* * 21. *Chameleon Planet* (with Philip Harbottle)

THE SHADOW PEOPLE

THE GOLDEN AMAZON SAGA, BOOK ELEVEN

JOHN RUSSELL FEARN

Edited by Philip Harbottle

THE BORGO PRESS

MMXIII

THE SHADOW PEOPLE

FIRST BORGO PRESS EDITION

Published by Wildside Press LLC

www.wildsidebooks.com

DEDICATION

For Dave Gibson

CONTENTS

THE GOLDEN AMAZON

by Philip Harbottle

In 1943 British writer John Russell Fearn decided to quit writing for the American pulp science fiction magazines, and to concentrate instead on books for the English market. Within a very few years he became established as a leading novelist in several genres, not only science fiction, but also mystery and detective fiction, and westerns.

His first new SF novel, *The Golden Amazon*, was published by World's Work in April 1944. In this story, a little girl of three years of age is made the subject of an idealistic scientist's illegal glandular experiments. The scientist's dream is to end world wars by creating a woman devoid of the usual lusts and frailties of mankind, who upon reaching maturity would institute a benign scientific rule. But the apparently successful experiment has a flaw: it instills into the girl a hatred for all men, and a ruthless cruelty. Her supernatural scientific gifts enable her to master atomic power, and practically leads her to destroy the world. She breaks the will and strength of men, and elevates women to positions of wealth and power. She also discovers human synthesis, and by this means she is able to escape retribution when she is eventually overthrown. She is seen to collapse and die, a victim of consuming ketabolism, echoing the memorable finale of Rider Haggard's *She*. In actuality, it was only her synthetic image, and this paved the way for the *Golden Amazon Returns*, and further sequels

Fearn sold reprint rights in the first novel to the prestigious Canadian magazine, the Toronto *Star Weekly*. The magazine carried a special Comics Supplement, the centre section of which was a 'complete novel', published in newspaper format. Aimed at a general readership, the novels were written by the top popular novelists of the day, including John Dickson Carr, Ellery Queen, and P. G. Wodehouse. They sold hundreds of thousands of copies, and the novels were syndicated to several American newspapers in the Maine and New York areas. The Amazon novels enjoyed extraordinary popularity (especially with Canadian housewives), and ran for the next sixteen years following the appearance of the first novel in the March 3, 1945 issue, ending with Fearn's sudden death in September 1960, aged only fifty-two. His final two Amazon novels appeared posthumously.

During Fearn's lifetime, only the first six novels were published in British hardcover editions from the World's Work in England, after appearing in the *Star Weekly*. This was because the publishers discontinued their entire fiction line in 1954. However, the Amazon novels continued to appear in the *Star Weekly*, eventually notching up twenty-four titles.

Fearn had resold paperback rights to the Canadian publisher Harlequin Books, but after publishing only the first three titles, they stopped publishing SF and other genre fiction to concentrate on their famous Romances line.

Meanwhile, as early as 1949, Fearn had realized that the Amazon series had the potential to run indefinitely. This presented him with a problem, however. The 'origin story' of the Golden Amazon was conceived and actually set during the Second World War. Subsequent novels were written during the war and the immediate postwar period, and projected their stories only a few decades into the future.

He very astutely realized that to keep ahead of reality, he needed to move the Amazon *further* into the future—first into the outer solar system, and thence to the stars. So with the seventh novel, he introduced a new main character, Abna of Atlantis—someone as equally intelligent, and even stronger than herself. These dynamics provided him with an *interstellar* canvas, thus ensuring that the series would remain ahead of reality.

Fearn's strategy was a great success, and the Amazon novels retained their popularity, ending only with his tragically early death in 1960. By then he had written a further twenty Amazon novels, and made preliminary notes for his next (which would later be written by Fearn's biographer, Philip Harbottle).

Long after Fearn's death, his entire Amazon series

would eventually see print from the pioneering US small press Gryphon Books in limited paperback editions, and later by the Canadian Battered Silicon Dispatch Box small press in their hardcover Omnibus series.

This new Borgo Press paperback series will be the first trade edition of all twenty-one of these later novels by Fearn, beginning with the seventh novel in the original series. First published in 1949 as *Conquest of the Amazon*, I have edited it slightly as *World Beneath Ice* (The Golden Amazon Saga, Book One) so that it can be read and enjoyed by new readers who may be totally unfamiliar with what had gone before. Subsequent novels have also been slightly edited for modern readers.

The publishers hope that this new series may create many more "fans of the Amazon." Meanwhile, any reader interested in seeking out the earlier six Golden Amazon novels will find that they are readily available on the internet, and in numerous earlier paperback and hardcover editions.

* * * * * * * * *

To date, readers can enjoy the following new Borgo Press editions:

Book One: *World Beneath Ice*

In destroying the threat of an alien invasion, the Golden Amazon had inadvertently caused a decline in the sun's heat, encasing Earth in an ice sheet that threatens to eliminate humanity. The Amazon encounters Abna, a descendant of Atlantis, stronger and even more scientifically advanced than she, and the ruler of an Atlantean colony still surviving in a protected environment on Jupiter. She refuses his offer of marriage, but agrees to form an alliance in order to restore the sun and save the Earth. One thing that Abna has not told the Amazon is that all the females of his race have been wiped out by a bacilli infection....

Book Two: *Lord of Atlantis*

A gigantic ridge of land rises from the Atlantic floor, causing massive tidal waves on either side of the ocean. Even stranger, both England and America are then assailed by an invasion of prehistoric monsters! A gigantic domed city rests on the newly risen plateau, whilst out in space an alien spacecraft orbits the Earth. Such are the mysteries and challenges facing the Golden Amazon, self-appointed governess of Earth, as she struggles to unravel the maze of mystery that was the deadly legacy of Atlantis!

Book Three: *Triangle of Power*

The marriage of Violet Ray Brant—better known as The Golden Amazon—and Abna of Atlantis should have ushered in an era of peace and scientific prosperity to the people of Earth. But an unexpected turn of events finds Abna betrayed and marooned on a satellite of Jupiter, and the Amazon flung far beyond the Solar System. With Earth's two protectors removed, the planet is now at the mercy of another Atlantean, the master scientist Sefner Quorne....

Book Four: *The Amethyst City*

The metaphysical union of the Amazon and Abna results in the mental creation of a fully mature daughter—Viona. Quorne, still struggling for domination, forces Viona into a marriage ceremony, and impregnates her. But with the intervention of Tarnec Brodix, a super-mind from an external universe, Quorne and Viona are separately flung into an ultra-dimensional limbo. Abna chooses to follow after his daughter, leaving the Amazon to brood over the disaster, alone in the Amethyst City of Saturn.

Book Five: *Daughter of the Amazon*

A miscalculation by the super-mathematician Tarnec Brodix destroys his universe, and the fault spreads into the Earth universe in the form of a Dark Tide of Absolute Nothingness. Unable to save himself, Brodix transfers his knowledge into the one mind powerful enough to receive it: that if Sefian, the son who has been born to Viona and Quorne. Sefian rapidly evolves, and, no longer human, after saving the Earth universe, vanishes into the greater universe, to seek new challenges. Then the Amazon is confronted with a further puzzle—a large section of the planet Neptune is discovered to be an exact duplicate of the Earth!

Book Six: *Quorne Returns*

The bacterial intelligences of Neptune plan to conquer Earth by replacing humans in key positions with alien duplicates. The Neptunians are themselves subjugated by the sinister Atlantean scientist, Sefner Quorne. Alerted to the threat, the Golden Amazon hits back by creating the ultimate doomsday weapon—only to precipitate a reprisal from the denizens of another universe....

Book Seven: *The Central Intelligence*

The Golden Amazon's arch-enemy, Sefner Quorne, discovers that all mental gifts, such as memory and creativity, are something that is broadcast throughout the universe by a Central Intelligence—and then interpreted according to the quality of the individual brain of the recipient. At the surprising suggestion of his wife, Viona, the Amazon's daughter, Quorne travels with her to the very center of the universe, in order to wrest the secrets of mentality from the very source itself!

Book Eight: *The Cosmic Crusaders*

The Golden Amazon renounces all ties with Earth when, together with her husband, Abna, and her daughter, Viona, she sets off on a journey to explore the cosmos. On the strange worlds of Alpha Centauri, she encounters Mizanu, the embodiment of evil—a planet-sized hypertrophied brain! Its baleful, crushing mental power threatens to reach out beyond the double-system of Alpha and Proxima Centauri to engulf the Earth and all the other inhabited planets of the galaxy—unless the Amazon can destroy it first!

Book Nine: *Parasite Planet*

The Cosmic Crusaders discover a fantastic world of mental parasites drawing form and substance from our own Earth, fifty light years distant. The planet is ruled by a being identical to the Golden Amazon herself—but an Amazon who's coldly scientific and vicious, mirroring the original Amazon as she had once been early in her career. Inevitably, they become locked in a deadly duel—to the death!

Book Ten: *World Out of Step*

The Cosmic Crusaders find themselves on a planet that seems mysteriously not to conform with natural law, a world out of step with the universe. It leaps ahead into time at unexpected moments, thereby suddenly adding many years of age to the flower-like inhabitants, and killing tens of thousands of individuals through death and old age. In trying to find the alien menace respon-sible, The Golden Amazon and her fellow Crusaders are flung backwards and forwards through time and space, threatening their own survival....

CHAPTER ONE
EMERGENCE

Here was the unbelievable. The highly trained scientific minds of the Golden Amazon of Earth, and her husband, Abna of Jupiter, were grappling with the completely unexpected—a vision such as they had never hoped to see; and now they did see it, they could not understand it.

The space machine in which they were traveling was nearly motionless. It hung in a lavender haze, an infinite space, in which there was no top or bottom. It extended to the limit of vision—and yet here and there were glittering stars, brightly scintillating points that suggested there were other worlds. Yet how could this be when occasionally across the vastness there marched the shadows of gigantic people—shadows so enormous that they plunged the space machine into eclipse every time they passed.

At last the Amazon stirred from the wonder of the view. She turned a face of phenomenal beauty and intelligence to the man beside her, and Abna, the seven-foot giant of Jupiter, merely shrugged.

"I don't understand it, Vi," he admitted. "We've

been in lots of queer places, but never one like this."

"There's Viona's space machine, anyway," the Amazon said, nodding to the infinity.

"Yes...." Abna relapsed into thought, swiftly going over the events that had led up to this singular experience.

Some time before, an enormously powerful nuclear bomb had been exploded. For some reason unexplained, its core had released a mysterious form of purple energy that had blown Viona—daughter of the Amazon and Abna—into an entirely different space. Now the Amazon and Abna had repeated the condition and they, too, were absorbed into this unexplained region. The only concrete thing they could hang on to was the fact that Viona's machine was not far away, moving against the pinpoints of the stars. Within the machine the girl herself was presumably alive, and Mexone, her husband, also.

"Try radio," Abna decided at length, and crossed to the instrument board. He spent a moment or two adjusting the controls and listening to the queer whistling note from the speaker.

"Abna calling Viona," he intoned into the microphone. "Can you hear me?"

There was a crackling of static, a wailing note, and then a reedy voice answered. It was unmistakably the voice of Viona.

"Dad! It's you? Where are you?"

"Approximately 2,000 miles away," Abna responded, looking at the instruments. "We can see you clearly as a moving speck despite the distance. I'll flash a signal light and maybe you'll be able to spot it."

He gave a nod to the Amazon, and she promptly pressed the switch of the single searchlight with which the machine was equipped. A brilliant light flashed on and off into the void, and immediately Viona's voice chattered again in the loudspeaker.

"Yes, I see it! Keep on flashing so I shan't lose you. What do I do now? Fly toward you?"

"Yes, you'd better do that. All four of us had better get together again. We're not going to achieve anything separately."

With that Abna switched off and crossed to the window to watch developments. The Amazon beside him, they stood surveying the lilac haze—the shadows of people crossing it occasionally—and in particular their attention concentrated on that tiny glittering speck which was Viona's space machine. Why it glittered when there was no visible sun was only one of the mysteries in this region. Light seemed to be transmitted brilliantly, but indirectly.

"There was something in that bomb which caused all this to happen," the Amazon remarked, as she watched the distant space machine slowly turn and head in their direction. "I'm just trying to think what it could have been. And it repeated twice, don't forget—once for Viona and Mexone, and again for us.... We've got to find out what happened."

"True enough, but it can wait until later. I want to find out something about this space to begin with."

The Amazon nodded, taking her eyes for a moment from the advancing space machine to the mysteries of infinity around her. She frowned as a titanic pair of legs came and went—shadows again, like the elongated shadows cast by a setting sun. They seemed to extend for infinite miles. For a moment she thought she had the solution, then it evaded her again.

The distant space machine grew. Abna waited until it was near enough to see the outlines clearly, then he crossed again to the radio and switched it on.

"Draw alongside," he instructed. "We'll put airlock to airlock and you can jump through. Okay?"

"Yes—okay," came Viona's young, eager voice. "Shan't be long now."

In that she was correct. When at last a dull thud and a slight quiver of the spaceship announced that contact was complete, Abna unfastened the somewhat old-fashioned airlock. Presently the airlock of Viona's machine was drawn into airtight contact by suction, and in a moment she and Mexone had made the easy leap from one machine to the other.

"Thank goodness for that!" Viona exclaimed, and threw herself into the Amazon's arms.

For a moment there was a tangle of golden and copper hair as mother and daughter embraced. Abna grinned, shook the big hand of Mexone, and then closed the airlock. In a few moments he was driving the machine away from the abandoned vessel, cruising to nowhere in particular.

"Well, what sort of a place are we in?" Viona questioned, turning at last and swinging to Abna's embrace. "Any ideas, dad?"

"I've had little time to formulate any. One thing I do know: this is a space we're not familiar with. Even the stars and constellations are cockeyed, aren't they, Vi?"

But the Amazon did not reply. She was again at the window, her unfathomable violet eyes contemplating space. She did not even seem to be aware there were others in the control room. Her extraordinary mind was given over entirely to the mystery of the surroundings.

"We've tried to figure it out, but we just get nowhere," Mexone said, as Abna glanced at him. "It was something to do with that exploding bomb we dropped— and that seems to be the limit of what we can discover."

"You weren't hurt at all when you were blown in this space?" Abna asked.

"Not at all," Viona responded. "Plenty of bruises, but we don't bruise easy. We were worried because we didn't know how to begin finding the way back. Now, of course, everything will be all right."

Abna smiled slightly. The superb trust the younger ones had in himself and the Amazon was something he did not accept lightly. He knew the responsibility, and was proud to wrestle with it.

"I may be wrong," said the Amazon at last, her voice slow and thoughtful, "but I don't think those stars are stars at all!"

"Then what—are they?" Viona asked hesitantly, her sapphire blue eyes full of wonder.

The reply was unexpected, yet to the point. "I think

they're lighted windows!"

"Windows?" Abna repeated. "How do you make that out?"

"Imagine yourself as a worm," the Amazon mused.

"Sometimes I am, in your estimation."

The violet eyes flashed reproof. "Don't go off into one of your 'little boy' moods, Abna. This is serious! I repeat, imagine yourself a worm, at night, looking up at the tallest building in London. You'd see lighted windows, spread out against the dark."

Abna looked long and earnestly, then he gave a low whistle.

"I believe you're right," he said slowly.

"There's another thing," the Amazon went on, "and that's the size of these shadow people. By comparison they would just be about normal if the stars we see are windows—normal, that is, for entry into one of the buildings."

"Could be," Viona murmured, also looking. "Have you got a theory about all this, mother?"

"Certainly I have. We all know that matter, when reduced to the last analysis, is basically a series of electrical charges with atomic spaces between. It is then visible only as a misty outline. To use an analogy— Look at a newspaper photograph from a distance, and it is perfectly normal. Look at it near-to and one sees an interspacing and the texture of the paper, with the picture only as a vague outline. So it is here.…" The Amazon paused for a moment, thinking. Then: "Long ago, in one of our experiences, we were plunged into the infinitely small, the region of atomic space. From that adventure we learned a good deal about relativity. That was an instance of being in the microcosm. I am wondering if perhaps there isn't a similar case here, only instead of being the microcosm, it's the macrocosm, the infinitely large."

"Meaning," Abna said at length, "that in our leap from normal space we extended infinitely and burst through the molecule which is our universe into an immensely greater one beyond? That being so, we are reduced to midget—indeed microscopic—size by comparison with our surroundings?"

"That is what I think has happened," the Amazon agreed. "And we can never hope to understand these shadow people, or gain the least conception of the space we're in, unless we, too, are of the same size."

"Which looks like being pretty well impossible," Viona said ruefully.

"There's radio though," Mexone put in quickly. "Surely it is possible that these people know what radio is? They might be able to contact us that way?"

"Perhaps...." Abna was thinking hard. "Don't forget that if this theory of a macrocosm is true, then a lot of other things are involved. Speech, for one thing. What is normal speech to us will just sound like so much chatter to them. On the other hand, their voices will be slow, sonorous, and generally unintelligible to our ears. Even apart from being an alien language."

"Well, I'm all for trying the radio anyway." Mexone hurried across to the radio equipment and switched it on. The Amazon, Abna, and Viona drifted slowly to his side and watched and listened intently. That the radio worked all right the Amazon and Abna knew full well, for they had, earlier, contacted Viona with the self-same apparatus; but whether it would establish any communication with the colossi was another matter.

After a series of preliminary whistles and squeaks from the loudspeaker, the power settled down to normal, and Mexone did the usual intoning into the microphone. Time and again he repeated the process, without any apparent effect. Finally he looked up with a frustrated glance.

"Waste of time, I'm afraid. No sign of a reaction."

"Leave the speaker open in case of response," Abna suggested. "Maybe these giants will require a little while to adapt themselves to our language. In the meantime, let's consider alternatives."

The Amazon gave a sharp glance. "Alternatives? What alternatives? There aren't any."

"There have got to be," Abna responded calmly. "You must have realized the position as clearly as anybody. Either we cruise around here in this ultra-atomic space until our food gives out and we pass away, or else we think up some way of blowing ourselves back into the normal space from which we came. Lastly, we have the alternative of increasing our size to that of the colossi. It may be dangerous to meet them; equally, it may not. But it won't be the first time we've taken a chance."

"You talk very freely about increasing our size to

that of the colossi," the Amazon remarked. "How exactly?"

Abna grinned. "I don't know offhand, but the mind should rise superior to any material problem."

The Amazon gave a dubious glance. Though she knew Abna was capable of the most incredible mental gymnastics, she always had this feeling of profound doubt beforehand. He had—to her—the irritating habit of making it all seem so simple.

"For the moment," Abna said, "let us see if our giant friends have any communication to send us. If not, we'll get busy."

"Assume a less difficult problem first," Mexpne suggested. "Supposing we decide to get back into our own space and leave this one forever unexplored. How do we do that?"

Abna brooded. The schoolboy-like smile had gone from his powerful features, and he was again the skilled superhuman scientist.

"Since we got here by the explosion of a particular type of bomb, we ought to get out the same way," he commented finally. "But there are other factors, since everything must now be reversed. It is a matter of implosion instead of explosion. We must be—"

"Say, something's happening out here!" It was Viona's suddenly excited voice. She was gazing out of the window on to the depths of atomic space, Mexone as ever by her side.

"Happening?" the Amazon repeated, turning. "In what way?"

"Come and look for yourself! The stars are growing bigger—or at least it looks that way."

The Amazon crossed to the window and Abna joined her. In puzzled silence all four stood for a moment surveying, and gradually it became apparent to them what Viona meant. The nearest 'pyramid' constellation of stars was undoubtedly altering shape.

"What's happening?" Viona asked breathlessly, and it was her father who answered her.

"I'll take one guess. That radio message we sent out was infinite in wavelength, not limited as was our message to you. Maybe it penetrated to the understanding of the colossi and made them realize that, although they couldn't answer, they could fix our position. Right now I'd say they've found us and are saving us a lot of trouble by enlarging us.... Yes," Abna added, with an intent study outside. "I'm sure of it!"

In a matter of seconds there was no longer any doubt of it. The shifting 'stars' changed position again and steadily grew larger, so much so that it finally became apparent that they were not stars at all, but, as the Amazon had guessed earlier, windows. Here and there across this lighted space there strode an occasional gigantic figure, but as the time passed, the giantism began to shrink and the stars assumed their normal aspect of windows in a truly tremendous building.

After that the transition from smallness to normality—if such it could be called—in a world gigantic beyond imagination was rapid. Suddenly the quartet within the space machine realized that everything had become still and that their vessel was standing in the center of an enormously long street, flanked on either side by buildings with a multiplicity of windows. It was night here, and out of the darkness an occasional figure walked, paused to stare in wonder, and then continued onwards.

"Apparently," Abna said finally, peering outside, "we've landed! It seems to be a main street of some sort. I assume the enlargement was done for us, but by what sort of apparatus has me guessing."

"Must be some kind of long-distance vibration for increasing the electronic orbits of ourselves and the ship," the Amazon commented.

None of the others attempted to question the rightness or wrongness of her theory: they were too busy gazing outside. As Abna had said, they had materialized in some kind of main street in a gigantic metropolis. The city sprawled for untold miles into the distance, ablaze with light and activity. Perhaps, though, this street was not a very important one, for vehicular traffic seemed to be nonexistent, and pedestrians were few and far between. The most interesting thing about the passers-by was the fact that they were comparatively normal when considered from Earth standards. In no sense did they have any leanings toward the grotesque.

"Well," the Amazon said at length, inspecting the weapon belt about her slim waist. "Do we venture outside, or wait for something to happen?"

"Since we are obviously under observation," Abna responded, "it seems it would only be common courtesy to wait for our friends to finish the job they've started. Besides, it will save a lot of time trying to explore. Something will happen soon."

The Amazon nodded agreement, gazing into the long vista of buildings. Her tremendously imaginative mind was finding it impossible to realize that here was a world so big as to be beyond belief—that she herself, Abna, Viona, and Mexone were really now so gargantuan that a million million earthly universes would fit inside their little fingers, and still leave infinite room.... Such a conception was impossible of realization, even though it was the mathematical fact. This was the macrocosm, never before penetrated.

"Looks as if somebody is coming," Mexone said presently. "See them—over to the right?"

The others looked intently. Some kind of vehicle was approaching at outlandish speed, apparently traveling in a deep groove, which now the quartet came to notice it, was gouged in the center of the road.

"Certainly traveling," Abna commented, as the queer, ball-shaped object leaped out of the distance.

"And incidentally, we're seeing the realization of something here which I've often theorized upon yet never seen actually. A monorail track."

Such indeed proved to be the case. Moving at certainly something in the neighborhood of 300 miles an hour, the vehicle shot nearer the motionless space machine. Moving with such speed it even occasioned the quartet a momentary alarm. It seemed it could never pull up in time, and yet it did. Stopping, it was only a matter of three yards from the stationary vessel.

"Well, this is it." The Amazon gave a grim glance as yet again she fingered the weapons in her belt. "I'm all set for trouble. How about the rest of you?"

"Why anticipate trouble?" Abna asked, with a curious glance.

"It's all one can expect. If the assumption proves to be incorrect, it's all the nicer.... Better get the airlock open, Abna."

He nodded, and the metal inner covering slid back. Then before opening the outer lock he suddenly bethought himself and consulted the exterior gauges over the switchboard. Not that he need have worried: the readings were quite reassuring, giving a temperature and humidity similar to that of Earth, and a breathable atmosphere. And, from the feel of things, gravity, too, was about normal, though with the change in size it was difficult to assess correctly.

"Talk about war paint!" Viona murmured, watching through the window. "Take a look at this lot!"

The others were already looking, and once Abna had the main airlock open he, too, crossed over to the window—to observe a quartet of resplendent individuals coming from the monorail ear. All of them were tall, but not abnormally so, with exceptionally wide shoulders. Every one of them was totally bald and clean-shaven, and their attire was magnificent to the last detail. Their robes seemed to be all in one piece and were of a delightful royal blue, with a deep sash of purple thrown over the left shoulder. They looked exactly like Scriptural dignitaries of extreme wealth. Nowhere did they appear to carry arms of any sort.

Abna raised a powerful arm in the universal greeting of goodwill as they came forward.

"Greetings!" Abna exclaimed, to break the tension. "We come as friends and to bring you good tidings."

For the first time the men smiled, not so much at the quartet as at each other. It seemed as though they had found the answer to a question that had puzzled them. Perhaps it was whether or not the quartet would prove hostile. Now they had their answer.

In response, one of the four men answered, but as had been anticipated, his language was completely incomprehensible. Finally he resorted to signs, indicating the monorail car with an unmistakable gesture.

"Do we?" the Amazon asked, with a glance, "If we lose this spaceship, we lose everything."

"We haven't much choice," Abna replied, shrugging, and set the example by walking forward. It pleased him to note that the four men fell aside in deference as he moved, and he even suspected their heads were slightly bowed in subservience. All of which did much to bolster up the theory of friendship.

Abna having taken the plunge, the Amazon, Viona, and Mexone followed suit. In a moment or two they were all within the control cabin of the monorail car, gazing about them with interest upon a number of panels that, from their very nature, proved that these people were anything but ignorant of scientific laws.

Entering, the leader of the four men waved to a long,

softly sprung seat. Then he and his colleague settled in special driving saddles and by automatic control the door closed. A second later the monorail car started up and, had the four not been accustomed to tremendous velocities, they would probably have been caused considerable anguish by the acceleration. Even as it was they were pressed tightly back into their sprung seats as with terrific speed the vehicle went back along the track the way it had originally come. The curious thing was that there seemed to be no lag between starting and picking up speed. Almost instantaneously the machine reached a 400-mile-an-hour velocity from a standing start, taking no cognizance of inertia or basic laws.

This was a problem that seemed to preoccupy Abna, and the Amazon, too, in a lesser way. She had not the mentality of an Abna, brilliant though she undoubtedly was.... Entirely disinterested in the scientific side issues were Viona and Mexone. Their heads close together, they gazed out of the window on the flashing scenery outside.

For a seemingly interminable time, despite their speed, there seemed to be nothing but the one enormous gouged road; but at last things began to change and they found themselves approaching the heart of the city proper. Then suddenly—stillness. Without any slowing down, or even a hint of it, the machine stopped dead. The quartet were thrown forward, but not as violently as they would have expected, but the four magnificently resplendent men seemed unconcerned as they climbed from their control saddles.

Abna, frowning, got to his feet and looked at the Amazon.

"First time I ever came across a vehicle that defied the laws of mass as this one does," he murmured. "Things don't seem to fit in the way we're accustomed to."

The Amazon nodded but did not say anything. She stood waiting as the four escorts opened the door of the vehicle and led the way outside, thereafter standing in deference for the travelers to follow.

"We're in it now," Abna said, shrugging. "Might as well go on with it."

He stepped outside and waited for the others to join him. As they did so, he gazed at the gigantic edifice before which the monorail car had drawn up. It towered up 200 and more storeys with the inevitable endless lighted windows. Significantly, there was an aircraft beacon on the roof, turning its yellow guiding light constantly to the skies.

"Evidently air travel is understood," the Amazon remarked, also seeing it. "Wonder if space travel is?"

"Soon find out," Abna murmured, as the four escorts started to walk forward, and presently up the wide steps of the building. Automatic doors slid aside.

Inside they crossed an immense hall, on the perimeter of which were several wide corridors. They followed their escorts into one of the corridors, then passed along it until they came to a room of tremendous proportions. In fact, it was more than a room; it had something in common with an electrical laboratory. There was, too, a hum of power and, from a great distance, the droning of dynamos. Over it all glowed the bright light of this world, though where it came from was skillfully hidden.

The leader of the quartet made a series of signals to signify that his part of the job was finished, and with a bow he retired with his colleagues and closed the platinum door. Abna turned from watching him go and gave a glance of inquiry.

"Well, what now, I wonder? And say, couldn't we do something with a lab like this, Vi?"

The Amazon seemed about to reply, then she paused as in the center aisleway a figure suddenly appeared—tall, bald-headed, and with an air of serene composure. He advanced silently.

CHAPTER TWO
MENTAL ONSLAUGHT

The four waited, not quite sure of what they ought to do. Then, rather hesitantly, Abna raised his arm in greeting, and to his satisfaction there was an immediate response and a broad smile of welcome. It was impossible not to like the newcomer. He radiated magnanimity, and at the same time imparted an air of supreme confidence.

"Greetings," Abna said gravely. "We haven't the least idea of your language—or, indeed, of where we are—but we come not as foes but as friends, anxious to exchange scientific information."

The man listened intently, his slender, capable fingers gently stroking the front of his violet one-piece uniform as though he were removing invisible specks of dust thereon; then when Abna had finished speaking he motioned for the four to follow him. They did so, rather wondering, and finished up in the center of a series of four machines. Complex things they were, the most obvious thing about them being the series of lenses with which they were fitted.

"Think the things are dangerous?" the Amazon

asked uncertainly.

"No reason why they should be," Abna replied. "Crazy though it may be, I'm quite prepared to trust our friend.… In fact," he added significantly, "we've little choice! Just try moving from this spot."

The Amazon started, then endeavored to walk forward. It was an effort that proved useless. She, and the others, were firmly rooted to the floor with their steel-shod shoes. Evidently magnetism of some sort was at work.

"I don't like it," she said grimly, her yellow hand flashing to her proton gun. "If anything happens—"

"Take it easy," Abna said calmly. "The man hasn't been hostile yet and we don't want to upset him before we've even started. We are probably anchored down for a very special reason—"

He stopped abruptly. Every light in the laboratory had suddenly extinguished. There was an intense silence. The four stood tensely waiting, their nerves taut—then abruptly the many lenses they had already glimpsed started to wink all manner of colors. The queer thing was that added to the known basic colors of the spectrum there were several others, quite impossible to describe in words—the type of colors that had to be seen to be understood. Then, quite abruptly, the lights snapped back into being. The four were left with an awareness of many things they had never known before.

"Greetings, my friends," said the tall, bald-headed scientist, switching off the color instruments. "My regrets if you were at all apprehensive, but since I could not speak your language, nor you mine, there was no way of warning you." He turned and smiled benevolently. "I trust you are quite comfortable?"

"Yes—quite," the Amazon answered slowly, wrestling with the fact that she found she knew the man's language as well as her own, and several other things besides. "You did alarm us for a moment."

"My apologies." The scientist gave a little obeisance. "If you will come this way I am sure you will be more comfortable."

He walked from the area of the machines, the four following him, and so through the wilderness of the giant laboratory to a fairly large anteroom. It was quiet and tastefully furnished—rather after the style of an Earth hotel lounge, and as usual there was the mystical hidden lighting.

"Do be seated," the scientist invited, drawing forth chairs. "Perhaps a little refreshment after your journeying?"

"That would be acceptable, but we're doubtful about it," Abna responded, sitting down. "Your food may not be suitable for our physique. Differences of origin, you understand."

The scientist laughed. "My dear Abna, why do you imagine the Readers went to work on you, your wife, daughter, and son-in-law? For the sole purpose of understanding your physique, mentality, and accomplishments. Have no fear. The food and drink will be entirely palatable."

He drew back the cuff of his tunic and uttered a few words into the tiny disc-microphone on his wrist, then he seated himself composedly and the smile of geniality never left his intelligent face.

"Do I need to introduce myself?" he asked politely, "or did the Readers do their work properly and transfer the necessary information into your minds?"

"Your name is Thorard, chief scientist of the planet Falsen," Abna answered correctly.

"Quite so. Your names, as you are aware, I know already. I am also conversant with many other things concerning you, but more of that later. I know of your journeying from faraway Earth, of your laudable endeavor to carry the knowledge and benefits of science to those races less fortunate in understanding. I know, too, of your unexpected penetration of our macro-space, so inconceivably large by comparison with your own." The slender hands moved in a gesture. "I was the first to be informed when you had penetrated here."

"You picked us up by our radio signaling?" the Amazon asked.

"Precisely. After that it was a matter of enlarging you to normal and then making contact. That was duly done."

"By what means?" Abna asked, and Thorard looked surprised.

"Surely that is not a problem to a man with your intelligence? All matter is composed of electronic orbits. The mass can be enlarged or lessened according to the width of the orbits. All we had to do was increase the orbits of yourselves and the ship you traveled in…and there you were!"

"With a space machine straddling one of your main roads!" Viona exclaimed, her blue eyes wide in interested wonder.

"The space machine *was* straddling one of the roads," Thorard smiled. "At the moment it is in the grounds of this laboratory, ready for when you require it. I had it transported here when you had left it."

Any comment on this was prevented by the arrival of refreshment. Indeed, it was akin to a many-course dinner and served on solid gold trays by silent, good-looking servants. Without any fuss or noise they set the meal out and then stood back to be on hand in the event of any little need. Thorard himself did not eat. He remained where he was, watching with a kind of tolerant amusement as the travelers satisfied their appetites.

"I would make it clear," he said presently, "that I am not by any means the ruler of this world. My job is purely that of a scientist, and I am responsible for all the scientific projects of this planet. In your case, of course, the matter fell directly into my province and I had you brought here. It will be my task to supply him with a full report."

"Of course," Abna conceded, between mouthfuls of food. "From all of which it would seem pointless to explain our purpose in being here. You know why already."

"In the main, yes. On the other hand, I am led to

believe you are here because you simply could not help it. Yours was not—shall I say—the achievement of a purpose. Your presence on Falsen is more or less accidental."

"Correct," the Amazon agreed. "All we wish to do is be friendly, learn something of your ways and habits as compared to ours, and then devise a means of departure once more to our own space.

"Quite so—quite so." Thorard rose from his chair and began to pace up and down slowly, his chin on his chest. Then after a while he looked up. "My friends, though I know so much about you, there is equally quite a deal which escapes me. Your science, for instance, is most peculiar—even more so your laws relating to mathematics."

"Oh?" Abna looked surprised. "Surely mathematics are the same wherever they are, in macrocosm or microcosm?"

"Apparently not. For instance, let us take the simplest form of multiplication. You would say two and two multiplied equal four, and that that answer holds good anywhere at any time."

"That is so, isn't?" Abna asked, puzzled. "Find any other answer and the whole principle of mathematics falls to pieces."

Thorard smiled a little. "In our space, my friend, the multiple of two and two is not four but five. On that basis our whole mathematical system is built. And, when you come to consider that, the matter becomes more complex as you delve deeper into mathematics, the discrepancy between your system and ours becomes gigantic. From that premise it would seem that you can never understand our mathematics, or we yours."

Abna frowned, looking inwards into the depths of his mind and upon the array of information that had been transmitted to him by the Readers. Undoubtedly Thorard had spoken truth. As far as mathematics was concerned, the planet Falsen was a dead loss.

"Yet neither system is at fault," Thorard hastened to add. "It so happens that whoever in the dim beginning conceived your principle of mathematics based the calculation of two and two to equal four. Here the assumption was five. The difference between our two intelligences can be glimpsed from that small fact alone."

The scientist stopped suddenly and put a hand to his forehead. The pleasant smile vanished from his face and instead it was replaced by an expression of tremendous strain. Even as Thorard staggered about the floor of the big room, fighting for control, the weird something that was affecting him also clamped down on the quartet. The Amazon sensed it first, like poisonous vapor creeping into her mind.

Their meal forgotten, the four sat fighting the horrible suggestions that were striving to master them. Thorard for his part was gripping the back of a nearby chair, his whole being thrown into one tremendous effort to beat the horror. So far he was succeeding— but for the Amazon the struggle was too great. Her mentality suddenly blanked out and with it went memory, reason, and every intelligent attribute. Not a second later Viona's mind snapped, too, followed in quick succession by Mexone and Abna.

None of them was aware of their actions, but an onlooker would have seen them snarling like animals, weapons forgotten, as they flung themselves at each other's throats in a life-and-death struggle.

Then, gradually, the unknown force began to relax—and relaxed still more. Thorard straightened up slowly, white and trembling. The Amazon felt as though a window had opened in a poisonous room and she was able to breathe again. By slow degrees the mephitic influence abated, and the quartet lay in the positions they had fallen, bleeding from their struggles, nerves temporarily shattered by the experience.

"My friends...my dear, dear friends." Thorard slowly staggered forward, gradually becoming himself again, perspiration dewing his bald head and drawn face. "I wish to heaven this had not happened. That you would not have been subjected to—it."

"What in the name of the devil was it?" Abna gasped getting to his feet. "From the look of things we have spent our time mauling each other."

He crossed over quickly to the Amazon and helped her to rise. She dabbed quickly at her bloodstained face and looked profoundly puzzled. Her eyes strayed to Mexone and Viona. They, too, were bruised and nail-scratched, and just as bewildered.

"We—we do not know what it is." Thorard motioned weakly to the chairs and sat in one himself. "I had hoped you would not have to experience it—or if it did come, I thought perhaps your type of physique and mentality would prove immune. Evidently I was—was mistaken. It has been happening for generations, according to our historical records. A strange, baleful influence from outer space that sweeps across our planet and for a brief while embraces every man woman and child. Its effect is to stir the emotions of the sexes against each other. Men desire only to destroy women, and women men. It has neither rhyme nor reason, but it is there. There is no defense against it, until—as in the case of myself, and one or two others who might be classed as higher types of mind—one builds up a resistance against it. The struggle is dire and dreadful and leaves one a physical and mental wreck for a while, but at least one is able to master the desire toward violence."

"And I suppose others are not so fortunate?" Abna asked, looking moodily at the remains of his unfinished meal.

"By no means. There is always a report of hundreds dead after the Wave has passed. Very soon now I shall know how many have died in this one."

The Amazon smiled gravely. "From the look of things, Thorard, you need not try just yet to work out a means of us getting home. It would appear that we have business here. And our first job is to locate the source of this menace."

Thorard shook his head slowly. "I'm afraid that will not be possible. We have done everything we can. What more is there to do?"

"A phenomenon like that can't happen without a cause," the Amazon answered. "And a very strong cause too. Perhaps you did not use the right instruments. Might I inquire what method you employed?"

"We used various means, but, of course, the difficulty was to remain sane or think clearly while the trouble was on. In the main we used a sensitive apparatus depicting mental strength. That gave a reading indicating a particularly high mental presence during the onslaught."

"You didn't use directional indicators?" Abna asked quickly.

"No." Thorard looked apologetically puzzled. "What are they?"

Abna smiled. "We use them a lot—perhaps a branch of science to which you are not accustomed. They will show us exactly where the trouble is coming from. We're not interested in the strength of it: we know already that it is considerable. Once we have pinpointed the source, we can perhaps do something."

"Yes, perhaps so." A new light of hope had come into the scientist's face. "We assume that it comes from outer space, but since we have no means of reaching outer space, there is nothing we can do about it—"

"But we can," the Amazon said grimly. "And we shall! A force so diabolical has got to be stopped, and it is part of our crusading endeavor to tackle such things."

"Tell me, Thorard, how often do these Waves occur?" Abna asked.

The scientist looked up and reflected. "In your figuring, about every month. Regularly as clockwork."

"Which means you must nave known it would happen when we were here?"

"I knew it was possible, but I naturally hoped you would avoid it."

"I see." Abna remained thoughtful. "Then we have another month before a Wave comes again?"

"If things happen as they have always done, yes."

"Right! That gives us a month in which to build a detector. It will mean the full resources of your laboratory, and we'd better do it ourselves rather than waste time in converting measurements to your own mathematics. Given reasonable luck, we'll be ready in time."

"True, but...." Thorard shrugged. "Have it as you will, Abna, and we are unspeakably grateful for the intercession of your science. The laboratories are at your disposal."

"That's all we need," Abna smiled.

"I gather you will be staying with us indefinitely then, and will not be seeking an immediate return home?"

"We'll certainly be staying until we've solved this problem," the Amazon answered.

"In that case I will make arrangements for your comfort and submit a full report to the ruler on your decision to help us. Possibly he will want to converse with you—"

"Be better if we don't have to take the time up," the Amazon interrupted. "Making a mental-wave detector in a month, and with a complete revision of mathematics thrown in, will demand every second of our time.... Afterwards, we'll have all the time in the world."

"So be it," Thorard assented. "You may rely on me and my fellow scientists to help you in every way possible."

CHAPTER THREE
THE SOURCE

Thorard was as good as his word, and by degrees the quartet found themselves settling down to the routine of their latest resting place and quite enjoying it, had it not been for the ever-present urgency of their endeavors.

Out of the chaos of the first stages there began to appear the highly sensitive detector which, for the first time, was going to show whence came the mysterious baleful Wave which was spelling menace and eventual doom to a quiet and extremely friendly race.

Finally there came the time, according to Thorard, when the supreme test would have to be made. According to his calculations the Wave was due again. For once the scientists were all keyed up in anxious excitement even if the populace was waiting in fear and trembling for an onslaught, which they knew they could not defeat or defend themselves against.

When there was only thirty minutes left to the time when the Wave was due, the travelers, Thorard, and a number of the planet's leading scientists took up their position in the laboratory to study out the phenomenon which was about to happen. They placed themselves at various points of the laboratory, watching monitor detectors connected to the main instrument.

"Stand by!" Abna ordered. "Here it comes.…"

The scientists braced themselves—and being prepared this time for what was to happen, Abna himself, the Amazon, and the two younger ones tensed their nerves and mentalities to the maximum of resistance.

Not that it was much use. Viona and Mexone were locked in combat on the floor, straining superhuman muscles to destroy each other. Abna and the Amazon were tearing and straining in a similar mad endeavor… then gradually, as before, the Wave began to relax and finally vanished, leaving behind it the bloodstained, scratched, and fiercely breathing quartet, and the quivering, slowly recovering scientists.

But the passing of the Wave had also left something else—a needle that had automatically stopped itself at the highest intensity of the onslaught, in the fashion of a stopwatch, and it was toward this that the party slowly began to move when they felt sufficiently recovered.

"A maximum intensity of 270," Abna remarked, with a grim glance. "That's a pretty strong mental power—"

"Pretty strong!" the Amazon exclaimed. "It's unbelievable. Even allowing for amplification, it's a tremendous force."

"True," Abna acknowledged. "So perhaps not a great

deal of blame attaches to us for going down before it. Now—direction is quite obviously above, but at an angle of seventy-five degrees. That means due south of the sky, according to our reckoning. And at a distance of—" He made quick calculations from the readings. "At a distance of forty-five million miles. About as far as Mars is from Earth."

"And what does that mean?" Thorard asked interestedly.

"Is it not obvious, my friend? The source of the Wave is located on a planet—or something like it—forty-five million miles distant to the south of the celestial hemisphere. The thing to do now is look for a planet in that approximate position."

"Probably Moyel," said one of the scientists, thinking.

"Moyel?" The Amazon glanced at him.

"Moyel is about the only planet in the southern sky. It is a practically unobservable world because of its perpetual cloud blanket, which hides the features of the surface. Come—we will show you."

Without delay the party retired to the great observatory, and though it was daylight—Falsen had a revolution of twenty hours, forty minutes—the huge master reflector had no difficulty in picking up the planet Moyel, probably because it was a world of extreme brightness, its clouds reflecting the distant sunshine with a relatively high albedo.

Having maneuvered the mighty instrument into position, the master astronomer stood aside and motioned to Abna. Promptly he settled down in the viewing-saddle and gazed intently through the binocular eyepieces.

Moyel loomed a bright, featureless world in an all-surrounding area of deep gray.

"There are no other planets or planetoids within the area, therefore that must be our objective. That is definitely established," Abna said.

"That is quite true," Thorard remarked. "Moyel, Falsen, and two other worlds far distant from us in the northern sky are the only ones in this system. We have long suspected that the Wave might come from there, and your detector has conclusively proved it; but we have never been able to do anything about it since we haven't mastered space travel. And even if we had, and reached Moyel, we would be overwhelmed by the Wave when encountering it at such close quarters."

CHAPTER FOUR
PLANET OF RUINS

There was silence for a moment in the observatory, then Abna spoke.

"That is a very good point you've taken, Thorard—the matter of the Wave becoming more intense as you come closer to it. We must take precautions against it."

"You mean you are actually going to journey to that world?" the scientist asked in astonishment.

"Certainly. There's no other way to get to the source of this Wave, is there? And we know it comes from there. I only wish we had our own space machine, the *Ultra*, with its array of weapons. We'd certainly give the perpetrators of this Wave something to think about."

"I do not like you venturing into such danger purely to save us. It isn't right—"

"It is when we have the knowledge of space travel and you have not. The destruction of your race by slow degrees isn't to be thought of. We're accustomed to danger, and besides, the mystery of the thing intrigues us.... The biggest problem will be to shield ourselves against the Wave at close quarters, though we ought to reach that planet and investigate it in well under a month—the time allowed before another Wave comes. On the other hand, there may be delay, and we don't wish to be caught. Any suggestions?"

"None," the scientists replied frankly.

During the ensuing silence the scientists looked troubled, as though they were personally responsible for the hold-up; then suddenly Mexone snapped his fingers.

"Look, Abna, thought-waves are basically akin to radio and television waves, are they not?"

"In a way, but infinitely shorter." Abna looked vaguely wondering.

"Well, then, maybe we're on the wrong track." Mexone's eyes were gleaming with the light of discovery. "We know that radio and television waves can be heterodyned, and even cut out and jammed entirely by an opposing wave. So why not thought-waves? We're not looking for an insulation against them, but something to entirely stop them having an effect."

"The boy's got something!" the Amazon exclaimed. "Interference! That's the answer. An electrical frequency sufficient to disturb the wavelength of thought waves! Let's get busy."

As was typical with the Amazon, an idea was instantly transferred to action. She wasted no more time in moving to the drawing boards in a quieter section of the laboratory, and the scientists of Falsen looked on in interested silence as the four argued with each other over the sketches they were executing.

Altogether, it took them some two hours to finally pool all their ideas into one and impale it on the drawing board, after which the design of the object they h»d planned quickly took shape.

"Understand it?" Abna asked, smiling, when the object was completed.

"Not entirely," Thorard confessed. "It looks like some kind of helmet."

"That's exactly what it is, and you might put in a mass job of constructing similar helmets for the populace. It will give them absolute protection. But of course that doesn't mean that the source of the Wave need not be destroyed.... To sum it up, the design of the helmet protects the receptive areas of the brain, those portions responsible for sight, sound, hearing, and so forth.

"A minute electric current is discharged from the battery you see here, which in turn is directed to this filigree of wires in the helmet. You will notice it is a kind of mesh. According to our calculations, the quality of the current will be exactly right for offsetting any thought waves that come in."

"Excellent," the scientist murmured. "Absolutely excellent!"

"Thank Mexone," Abna replied. "It was his idea in the first place. There is, however, one drawback."

"And it is?"

"Ordinary conversation between we four will be impossible, because, once we reach Moyel, we shall not dare to raise the ear coverings. Our only course is personal radio, so that our heads are never for a moment left unprotected." Abna tossed down the drawing pen with an air of finality. "How long will it take to manufacture four helmets to this specification?"

"Twelve hours. Certainly no longer."

"Good! See to it right away, Thorard, and we will stock up the space machine with everything needful, including the best ammunition you've got. The sooner we get on the way, the better. We want to do as much as possible before the next Wave is due."

* * * * * * *

Thorard was as good as his word, and the following morning the four completed helmets were duly delivered.

"That's all we need," Abna said in delight, trying his helmet on. "We're safe enough to venture—and if it comes to that, we have no reason to delay any longer. We have nothing to do but thank you for your hospitality, Thorard."

The bald scientist smiled slightly. "The hospitality is nothing, my friends—a very small thing compared to the risk you four are taking on. Obviously it is useless to try and deter you, so as an alternative accept our profound gratitude. We shall be anxiously awaiting your return."

"And while you're waiting for that," the Amazon said, "mass produce these helmets for your people. All those wearing them will be immune from the next Wave, if there is a next Wave. We hope to have destroyed the source of it by then."

The scientist nodded and thereafter accompanied the four to the area of open park surrounding the great edifice, where lay the fully prepared space machine. Without further comment Abna led the way into the vessel, looking back from the airlock when the Amazon, Viona, and Mexone had joined him.

"May the God you believe in watch over you," Thorard said quietly. "We will pray, too, to the God of our belief."

"So be it," Abna replied, and with that he closed the airlock and crossed to the control board. Here he paused a moment and picked up his helmet. He glanced at the Amazon, then to Viona and Mexone.

"In case of unexpected trouble, we'd better wear these all the time, and communicate with each other by radio. We'll be all right with the receivers fixed on our ears. Okay?"

The others nodded silently and proceeded to strap their helmets into place. Once this was done, Abna settled at the control board and started up the space-ship's engines. In a matter of moments the machine was lifting swiftly from the broad deserted reaches of the park below into the dense blue of the morning sky.

Thereafter it was the usual game of waiting and sleeping as the lazy, useless hours passed by. For each one of them it was a grueling job to have to do nothing—and space travel as such was no longer a novelty to intrigue the imagination. All they could do was speculate upon the possibilities of Moyel, until at last, swathed in vapors, the planet filled all the void ahead.

Finally, the machine dived into the swirling mists, swept quickly through them, and emerged into the twilight grayness of late afternoon. Each of the quartet was somehow expecting the unusual, bearing in mind the Wave and its baleful effects. Their surprise was therefore absolute when they beheld nothing more intriguing than normal landscape—partly bare rock and partly trees, with an ocean in the far distance upon which no vessel was apparent.

"Looks like a near-dead world," the Amazon remarked finally. "Yet that it can't be in view of what's happened. Better make a complete circuit of the globe, Abna, and see if there's anything else. Of course, any space traveler landing in Earth's Sahara might assume the planet was dead."

Without commenting, Abna obeyed instructions. With smooth, resistless speed the flyer swept over the landscape, always with dense cloudbanks above. Once, even, during this process the clouds deepened to midnight blackness and within seconds an electrical storm of phenomenal violence was playing around the spaceship. So great was its speed that it was through the storm area within a matter of minutes, but that did not make the onslaught any the less terrifying.

It became apparent that there were ruins below, most of them hedged round with fairly tall, completely wild jungle. There were tremendous terraces, such as must have once been superb in their architecture, which were now nothing but masses of slag and tumbled columns.

"Nothing to be gained by the tour of inspection," Abna said finally. "We'd better land."

Since the Amazon raised no objections he brought the vessel round in a long, sweeping curve and finally descended in what had once plainly been a broad and magnificent square. Now it was a smashed ruin, flanked on all sides by tall, queer-shaped trees that formed the basis of an incipient jungle.

The humming of the spaceship's engines ceased and Abna looked round from the switchboard. Viona was the first to comment.

"For a planet which transmits such deadly forces it's remarkably quiet," she observed. "Wonder if it's some kind of trap? I half expected to find a world bristling with a scientific metropolis, and all we get are a lot of trees, weeds, and broken stone."

"Better explore," Abna decided finally. "We can't see things clearly enough from the air. The fact remains that the Wave does come from here and it's our job to find out where."

The Amazon tightened the strap about her helmet and inspected the weapons in the golden belt about her waist. For some reason her highly sensitive mind was disturbed. She could sense very real danger before it became apparent—a gift which was perhaps something entirely exclusive to her sex.

Abna paused only long enough to study the exterior gauges—which showed the atmosphere to be comparatively normal by Earthly standards—then he unfastened the airlock and swung it open, taking his first appraisal of this strangely silent, deserted world.

"Let's go," Abna said decisively, and led the way into the open.

In a moment or two the Amazon, Viona, and Mexone had caught him up. Gradually they progressed, keeping a wary eye on the space machine so they would have no difficulty in reaching it again.

Around them loomed the relics of a once mighty civilization, and the ever-intrusive weeds. Then presently Abna glanced at the sky.

"Seems as if the wind action on this planet is all confined to the upper heights," he remarked. "Nothing seems to be happening down here, yet look at those clouds!"

"That's not a natural climatic effect," the Amazon commented finally. "It looks as though the atmosphere is being reacted upon from outer space, though exactly in what manner I can't say."

Then, as the slow, fruitless progress continued, Abna glanced again at the sky.

"What do you make of that?" he asked, and the Amazon contemplated the gathering blackness with a wry face.

"A storm, obviously. And from the look of things, a pretty violent one. We ran through one while circling the planet, remember? Perhaps we'd better get back—"

She had hardly spoken before a brilliant fork of lighting flashed down the sky. Hardly had it hit the ground before the thunder followed it—and what thunder! It made the very ground shake with earth-quake force and deafened the quartet as they stood in astonishment deciding what to do.

They dived for shelter, what little they could find of it. Finally they huddled, drenched to the skin, under a vast ledge of stone that had probably once been some kind of veranda. Amazed, and not a little startled by the suddenness of everything, they peered through the cloudburst at the cascades of purple light streaming from the midnight sky. All around them, between the very short intervals between thunder cracks, they could hear stonework and trees snapping and rending under the bolts of lightning—and around their feet water began to flow steadily, carrying with it a cloying, sticky ooze.

"Delightful spot," Abna said at length. "Looks as though the climate's completely haywire in this place. By no possible stretch of imagination could I call this a violent thunderstorm—or even a tropical one. It's like a demon let loose!"

Such indeed it proved to be as, for nearly an hour, it roared and exploded with appalling fury. Twice the stone ledge under which the four were sheltering was hit by lightning, producing an immense fissure in the stone—but it did not collapse. The whole area seemed to have changed to a wilderness of swirling water and unleashed electricity—then suddenly, nothing.

By degrees Abna dragged himself from the mud and water and emerged from under the ledge. He looked up at the sky. The midnight blackness had gone and the old swirling gray was there. Not a drop of rain was falling and there wasn't even any evidence that the storm had moved further on. It had simply disappeared.

"Wonder if storms like this are very frequent?" Viona gave an uneasy smile as she, too, came out into the open—and in another moment she was joined by her mother and Mexone.

"Going to make the going tough if they are," Mexone said, a puzzled look in his eyes as he noticed the sky's abrupt return to normal. "The climate doesn't behave as any self-respecting climate should."

"As a matter of fact," the Amazon said slowly, "I don't think it was a storm at all."

The three turned and looked at her, half astonished.

"Then what was it?" Abna asked.

"It was a perfect example of a weakened magnetic field. The sudden start and equally sudden stop. A sudden bursting forth of an electrical area, which had reached the limit of its potential load and had to break down. The moment it had done so, it ceased, and the dense nimbus cloud produced by the phenomenon simply evaporated."

"I believe," Abna said slowly, "that you're right, Vi. Which is why the planet is deserted. It will finally be destroyed anyway by the cosmic storms. Every planet has a magnetic field, and once weaken or destroy that and it is as unprotected as an orange without its skin.... It's a grim thought," he finished, frowning.

"And it doesn't help us to understand how a Wave machine could work from here," Viona put in. "Or have we forgotten all about that with the things that have been happening?"

"We have not forgotten anything," Abna assured her. "We are simply discovering some grim facts on the way, pointers perhaps as to the kind of civilization that once existed here."

"Once existed?" Viona repeated. "What about the Wave?"

"As to that, it could easily be automatically controlled. It wouldn't be the first time we've come across posthumous scientific gadgets, still operating generations after the inventors have passed away. We've got to find it, and we stay here until we do. The people of Falsen cannot continuously rely on protective helmets."

"Let's be moving then," the Amazon said. "We've wasted enough time as it is."

She took a few strides forward, and that was all. Suddenly, from the midst of the ruins and dripping vegetation springing up among them, there appeared a group of men. They were very small, ferocious-looking, and brown-skinned. The creatures, who had evidently been hiding from the storm amidst the ruins, abruptly sprang into life again and hurled themselves forward. Before the quartet had even a chance to draw weapons they found themselves in the midst of tearing, claw-like nails, sharp teeth, and super-strong bodies. Some of the attackers were men, and some women; that fact was briefly noticeable—and it was also noticeable that the women flung themselves savagely at Abna and Mexone, while the Amazon and Viona went down before the onrush of the men.

In a moment a desperate struggle was in progress. The quartet lashed out with their fists with all the tremendous strength they possessed. Pygmies collapsed in various directions, either dead or with broken limbs, but this seemed to make little difference. They still came in droves, thicker and thicker out of the jungle and ruins—the women always heading for the men, and the men for the women.

The Amazon and Viona for their part found themselves flattened into the ooze and filth before they could save themselves. They lashed out savagely at leering, vicious faces, kicked with their heavy space boots, used their muscular power to every possible advantage. But it was the very numbers that overpowered them. To fight a constant dozen pygmies at once was impossible. In the end the Amazon found herself pinned face downwards in the mud, very close to choking, her arms wrenched up behind her and four men apiece seated on her legs whilst strong vines were bound around them.

She struggled savagely, desperately, but all to no avail. In the end both she and Viona were tied immovably. Only then were they hauled to their feet, caked in mud and gasping for breath.

For Abna and Mexone things had apparently fared even worse. They lay stretched in the mud without a sign of movement, a group of pygmies dancing around them. For a moment they looked like two dead Gullivers. Dead? The Amazon gave a shout of horror.

The Amazon and Viona stared dully, then they were

prevented from seeing anything further as they were suddenly whipped around and lifted shoulder high. In another moment they were being borne along quickly amidst the ruins and vegetation, leaving Abna and Mexone where they had fallen.…

CHAPTER FIVE
THE PYGMY GIRL

Darkness came swiftly on Moyel. No twilight, no anything—just night, like the turning off of an electric light switch. And with the darkness Abna moved slowly in the sticky, drying mud and began to pick up the threads of life again. He lay for a long time trying to piece together what had happened. He closed his eyes, and for a while was not Abna, the flesh-and-blood being of Jupiter, but a purely mental concept in the sea of infinity. It was rarely Abna took the trouble to lift his superb mind to such heights, but in an emergency he had no other course—and on this occasion, as on others, he gradually resumed normalcy in regard to his physical condition. Gradually his various injuries ceased to be. Where an ordinary man would have lain there in the mud to die, Abna rose superior to the material conditions and finally stood up, drawing deep breaths of air into his massive chest and flexing rippling muscles.

Suddenly he thought of Mexone and moved around quickly in the pitchy darkness and mud until at last he found him, hardly breathing, his face and head sticky with something else beside mud. Accordingly, he lifted his mind again above the physical conditions, this time for Mexone's sake, and in a few minutes the younger man began to recover, and finally stood up with Abna's powerful arm to help him.

"What—what happened?" Mexone's uncertain voice sounded in Abna's earphones.

"Happened? Well, from the look of things we were left for dead—but we're not so easy to kill. How long ago it was I don't know, but the night's come since. Where Vi and Viona are I just don't know."

Mexone felt at himself. He could detect dried blood, but on the other hand he felt remarkably fit and healthy,

"Now, let's see," Abna said finally, and managed to pull a mud-clogged torch out of his waist belt.

He cleaned the glass, and the tiny atomic battery operated the instant he depressed the switch. A brilliant beam stabbed into the darkness of the Moyelian night and revealed the ever-present jungle and ruins… but nothing more.

"Vi!" Abna called sharply. "Vi—Viona! Are you around?"

Abna strode forward in no particular direction calling as he went. Mexone shouted, too, but the empty spaces only gave back his voice for echo. The pair of them had gone about a dozen yards when Mexone suddenly stopped.

"What about the spaceship?" he asked in consternation.

"Well, what about it?" Abna asked. "I suppose it's

still where we left it, but we've no time to start tracing it now—"

The remainder of his sentence was wiped out by a crash of thunder that made the landscape rock. Simultaneously with it came a jagged fork of lightning that seemed to literally explode out of the black heavens, flaring everything for a brief second in the brightest lavender.

"Another one!" Mexone groaned. "Isn't there ever a let-up in this place?"

Apparently there was not. In perhaps thirty seconds a storm, every bit as violent as the one that had preceded it, burst in all its fury. Abna and Mexone staggered on, sometimes arm in arm—until with unexpected suddenness they floundered into the midst of some kind of fast-moving river.

Abna was aware of one thing as he swam mightily, and it gravely disturbed him. His wrist compass was smashed to pieces. It had happened when he had taken his plunge into the river, striking his wrist on an upstanding piece of stone as he had done so. It had saved his wrist from damage, certainly, but the loss of the compass was a tragic thing.

Abna was debating this mishap, and studying the opposite bank between the savage flashes of lightning, when he fancied he heard a cry. It was the cry of a doomed person—a hysterical scream for assistance.

He looked about him quickly—and Mexone, who was not far away, looked also. For a time neither of them could observe anything in the smothering downpour, then another of those intensely bright lightning flashes ripped the sky, the trailing ends of the fiery streamers striking the opposite bank. In that snapshot-like lilac glare, Abna caught a glimpse of a brown object bobbing helplessly in the yellow river, and not very far away either. Instantly he gave a shout to Mexone and struck out towards it. Traveling now with the current, and aided by a strength that was super-human, he covered the distance in a few seconds and grabbed hold of a nearly drowned woman pygmy. She made no attempt to struggle, and submitted passively to his gripping hands.

Again the battle broadside to the current. Then Mexone came swimming up and lent his assistance. Between them they managed finally to reach the shoals of the opposite bank and carried the pygmy out of danger's reach and laid her down.

The storm stopped—instantly. Without any less-ening of fury, without any hint of change, it ceased. The lightning and thunder were gone and rain stopped. Abna knelt, breathing hard, his torch in action again. Water did not in the least interfere with its action. The powerful beam cast upon the half-dead woman, attired in the usual breast-high costume of cheap fabric, which stopped short just above her knees. Curiously, she was not quite so ferocious-looking as the other females who had made the earlier attack. Indeed, she even had a claim to looks.

"Well, what now?" Mexone asked grimly. "Leave her here to recover? I've no particular love for these people, Abna, and we've got work to do."

"I've got a sort of hope that she may be able to help us," Abna responded. "She must know more about this infernal planet than we do.… Just a moment."

He switched off his torch beam and became motionless. Mexone, who was accustomed to such a performance, waited impatiently, wondering what the idea was. Then, when the torch clicked on again he stared in wonderment as he beheld the pygmy girl entirely recovered. At the arrival of the light she raised herself on one elbow and peered with big dark eyes into the glare.

"Doesn't seem much the matter with her, considering," Mexone remarked in surprise. "I thought she was nearly dead."

"She was, but we've put that behind us," Abna replied calmly; then leaning toward the girl he asked deliberately: "Do you understand my language?"

She frowned, a mystified light in her eyes as though she had just discovered something. With an effort her lips formed a reply:

"Yes, I understand your language. I do not know why I should do, but it has suddenly come upon me."

"Good," Abna smiled; then he caught sight of Mexone staring at him amazedly. "Don't let it worry you, Mexone. I found this girl's mind very tractable. It was simple, at the time I destroyed the effects of near-drowning, to also transfer to her a knowledge of the English language. When one is in the purely mental plane, all such matters are easy. One day, perhaps, you will have attained to such heights."

"Maybe," Mexone agreed, though he looked as if he doubted it.

"You do not know us any more than we know you," Abna resumed, putting his arm about the girl's shoulders as she struggled to her feet. "We are of different worlds, and seek to be friends. Apparently your colleagues don't feel the same way. They left my friend here and I for dead, and have kidnapped my wife and daughter."

"They would be the Ajipurs," the girl said, thinking.

"I take it, then, that the Ajipurs are of a different race to yourself?" Abna asked.

"Same race, different grade of intelligence." The girl seemed to be getting a grip on herself, and her mastery of the language was rapidly taking shape. She looked curiously at the helmets Abna and Mexone were still wearing and then continued: "Naturally the lower grade of intellect succumbs before the higher. I am of the Ijons, the once-ruling caste. Hence I have a higher intelligence and a greater refinement."

"I see." Abna puzzled it out for a moment or two, then he smiled. "I think I understand. You mean that, because you are of a higher intelligence, you do not relapse into the bestial ferocity of the lower grades? The relapse into bestiality is caused entirely by mysterious mental waves that sweep over this entire planet, is it not? Do you know what we are discussing?"

"Yes, I understand you. You speak of the Mind, which has destroyed our civilization."

"Destroyed your civilization?" Abna repeated, interested.

The girl moved a little. "Let us get to somewhere more comfortable, then perhaps I can explain."

"I'm quite agreeable," Mexone said, as Abna moved, "but what about Viona and your wife? We haven't found them yet."

"A few more minutes or hours can't make much difference," Abna said. "Perhaps this young lady can help us."

"If there is any way I can help you, I will," she said promptly. "It is but a small return for your saving my life in the river there. But come...."

She turned and headed with unerring sense of direction into the darkness. Then seeing Abna was uncertain of his way, even with the torchlight, she turned and took his hand. In turn Abna took Mexone's, and so they progressed.

They left the area of the river entirely, went quickly over an intervening stretch of sticky mud, and then came surprisingly upon a kind of compound, made up entirely of mud dwellings after the fashion of old-time African savages. Obviously they were tenanted. The area was lit with spasmodically burning torches stuck at various intervals in tall posts. Here and there men and women, roughly and cheaply clad, emerged from the dwellings, stared at the newcomers, and then retreated without asking questions.

Finally the girl led the way to one of the mud huts and passed inside it. One of the inevitable torches, giving forth a haze of sweet-smelling smoke, provided a light of sorts and cast upon squat, roughly made furniture, a bed, and one or two faded rugs.

"My home," the girl explained, without shame. "Do rest a while if you can find somewhere."

This was simple enough. Abna, because of his immense height, sprawled on the floor with his massive legs tucked under him, while Mexone took refuge in one of the chairs.

"Food?" the girl asked, bringing forth a bowl of fruits from a rickety cupboard. "This is all we have here. I was out picking some from the jungle trees when I fell into the river."

Abna took some gratefully, and Mexone followed suit. The girl, too, ate some, then put the bowl back and settled herself on the edge of the crude bed.

"This habitation of dried mud is all that remains of a mighty scientific city which once covered our planet," she said sadly. "I make no apology for it. It is just one of those things. The people who live here with their children were once the reigning dignitaries of the planet, myself among them. Now we're reduced to semi-savagery, always at the mercy of three things—the Mind, the ferocious attacks of the Ajipurs—as we call the less intelligent survivors—and the storms. Finally there must be an end. The Mind will destroy us."

"What is this Mind?" Abna asked.

"The Mind is a gigantic thought amplifier. There was at one time a danger of war from a small and insignificant race on this planet. War had not been known for centuries, and our scientific experts were determined to stop it, but not by open hostilities. To have done that would have placed them in the wrong. What they did was to create mechanical mind impulses, designed to react in two different ways. One affected the more sensitive female mind, and the other the male. It was planned that the male would destroy the female and vice versa. For a time it worked perfectly, the hostile race destroyed itself. But the machine somehow absorbed power out of space—cosmic energy, I think the scientists called it—and it became a menace in that it spread its area of power. It did it so rapidly that nobody could find a means of insulation against it before it had every man and woman on the planet in its grip. The result was devastating war, the battle of the sexes. Our cities and science were destroyed, our atmosphere weakened, exposing us to cosmic energy storms, and the Mind lived on—buried somewhere under the rubble of the cities."

"So that is the explanation," Abna said slowly. "How is it that you survive the Mind's continuous outpourings?"

The girl shrugged. "Presumably we have built up a certain resistance to it and so we manage to survive. That it does influence us is obvious because, as I say, we have not the intelligence any more to rise out of the squalor and semi-stupor into which we have been plunged. Someday, perhaps, a person with a mind stronger than the rest will lead us."

"Do you know what is meant by a month, or four

weeks?" Abna asked.

"I have some conception of it as a length of time."

"Can you remember if the Mind seems to be more powerful at monthly intervals than is normally the case?"

The girl reflected, then shook her head. "It does not seem so to me. It has about the same numbing strength always—constantly."

It was Mexone who provided the answer. "There is perhaps a simple explanation for that, Abna. Perhaps the world of Falsen swings nearer to Moyel every month, in the course of its journey, and accordingly receives a greater overflow blast from the Mind. As we know, it travels rapidly in its orbit—very rapidly."

"Yes, that may be the answer," Abna mused; then, as he realized the girl was listening in surprise, he explained the circumstances to her.

"Then you are of this world of Falsen?" she inquired.

"No. We are merely trying to help them out of their difficulty—which is your difficulty, also. We are out to destroy the baleful influence of the Mind somehow. We are not of Falsen, but of worlds far beyond this space, indeed in another universe. It would take too long to explain. There are two women in our party—my wife and daughter, who were captured by the Ajipurs, and we are desperately anxious to find them. I could perhaps get some lead on them telepathically, but to do so would mean removing my helmet, and that might be fatal since I am not inured to the Mind at such close quarters. Have you any suggestion to offer?"

"The main base of the Ajipurs is some distance from here, in the heart of the jungle. Perhaps your wife and daughter have been taken there. I can guide you if necessary."

"That is all we ask," Abna replied. "Incidentally, what is your name?" he asked.

"Marita." The girl smiled faintly. "I once had a long title, but it doesn't matter any more...." She got to her feet and went over to the door of the hut, gazing outside. For a moment or two her slim figure was silhouetted against the graying opening.

"It is coming daylight," she said. "We can be on our way any moment you choose."

CHAPTER SIX
LEFT TO DIE

Meanwhile, things were not exactly comfortable for the Amazon and Viona. With the firm belief that Abna and Mexone had been killed, much of their courage deserted them. Resourceful though they both were to the highest degree, the apparent loss of Abna and Mexone, and the spaceship as well, produced an immense depression of the spirits. Nor could they do anything to help themselves. They were borne along roughly through forest and ruins alternately in the grip of the ferocious pygmies.

Finally the journey through darkness ended, and they were borne into a region of increasing light. Only when they were set on their feet did they behold the real extent of this community of savages—for such indeed they were. In this case the inhabitants seemed to be all men, little and ferocious beings, who swept forward to paw and examine the captives. The little horrors seemed to be everywhere.

They found themselves eventually being tied to two enormous posts, and as before, the pygmies made a thorough job of the vines and knots. When they had finished, neither Viona nor the Amazon could move a fraction of an inch. Satisfied with their handiwork, the little men retreated to a distance as though watching for something to happen.

"Wonder what the idea is?" the Amazon questioned. "I thought they'd kill us. These posts are solid copper, obviously the pinnings from some ancient building—"

"I've got it!" Viona cried, sudden alarm in her voice. "I know what the idea is—and it's horrible."

"What?" The Amazon turned her head.

"These posts are copper, you say—"

"They are. I noticed it just before we were tied to them."

"And—" Viona strained her head to look upwards. "And they rise to about fifty feet. Can you imagine what will happen if one of those storms breaks loose? Copper is a perfect electrical conductor."

"We've got to get away," the Amazon said at length, with the cold determination that so often characterized her. "If we tear all the skin off our bodies, we've got to get free of these vines! It's certain death otherwise. If we can get free without attracting too much attention, we've room in which to escape. Try your hardest...."

Thereupon she filled her lungs with air and then began the enormous effort of muscular strain, which she hoped would result in freedom. There was a click, and one vine gave way. Encouraged, the Amazon tried again. Perspiration began to roll down her face in streams as muscles and tendons gave forth all their strength. And more vines snapped. At the same moment, Viona, hardly less powerful than her fabulous mother, also succeeded in breaking two of the most powerful tendrils clamping her legs.

Again and again—and in the dim light the little men could not see what was going on. Their captives, so they thought, were still secured immovably—but they thought differently when the Amazon, exerting enough strain and pressure to burst a blood vessel, suddenly pitched forward as the main vine around her legs and arms suddenly gave way. Instantly she recovered herself, tore the rest of the vines away, and darted to help Viona.

It was the signal for a mighty roar of fury to escape the pygmies, but this time the Amazon was ready for them. More, they had a distance to cover before reaching her. She turned, wrenched out her protonic gun, and opened the flame-nozzle to its widest capacity.

How the battle would have gone amidst the racing hordes was a question, but suddenly it was interrupted by the same storm that had caught Abna and Mexone. Lightning whiplashed the sky from three places simultaneously and the ground heaved under the belching roar of the thunder. The effect on the pygmies was extraordinary. They fled and bolted in all directions, like ants in the midst of which somebody had dropped a lighted match. Suddenly—amazingly—the Amazon and Viona found themselves without enemies.

"Well, that's something—" the Amazon started to say; then the blast of the storm took the rest of her words from her.

A truly amazing electrical deluge descended from the black heavens upon the copper posts. For a moment they glowed like the columns of Hades and then became blank again—but the frightful power of the flash ripped along the ground and flung the Amazon and Viona from their feet. Even as they crashed down they were aware of the lightning stripping them and tearing the helmets from their heads. At the same instant they were numbed by a tingling paralysis. For several seconds they just lay there—stupefied.

"The helmets!" the Amazon cried suddenly, in horror. "Find the helmets!"

Immediately she was on her feet, the paralysis passing. The helmets had vanished in the smother of rain and mud. Finally the Amazon stopped, took a deep breath, and closed her eyes.

"You feel it?" she whispered. "The effects of the Wave, or whatever it is?"

"I feel it," Viona assented, trembling. "It's getting worse all the time…. Mother, what are we going to do? Without those helmets there's no telling what might happen to us."

"Concentrate against this thing!" the Amazon insisted. "It's our only hope."

But normal conception abruptly stopped. They were completely under the mastery of the Wave. They began moving again toward the jungle—no longer resembling two highly-developed products of a streamlined scientific age, but more after the fashion of predatory animals, half-crouching, a mindless blank in their eyes, their senses completely unable to absorb anything of what was happening around them. Thunder, lightning, and rain meant nothing to them. They did not even start when lightning struck the ground a few feet away from them. Nor were they in the least concerned when the storm abruptly ceased. They went on through the night, searching for male prey, two women utterly transformed.

CHAPTER SEVEN
THE BARRIER

Through these same storms and peaceful periods Abna, Mexone, and Marita moved tirelessly through jungle and shattered cities alike. To the two men it was a completely unfamiliar journey. They had lost all hope of ever trying to find their spaceship again. Their sole concern was to find the Amazon and Viona, if they still lived, and then pool their resources in thinking up some way to get out of their difficulties.

Marita, for her part, seemed to have a pretty accurate knowledge of where she was heading—presumably toward the abode of the Ajipurs—the pygmy men. When it was finally reached, she stood gazing in speechless dismay at a smashed wilderness of mud huts, in the midst of which morass stood two tall copper pillars.

"I— I never expected this," she said haltingly, and looked up in dismay at Abna.

"This is where you expected to find my wife and daughter?" he asked quietly.

"Yes. Or at least some information concerning them. The storms seem to have destroyed everything."

"What's that?" asked Mexone abruptly, pointing. "Those two things sticking out of the mud. They look like—"

He did not wait to finish his own sentence. Diving forward quickly, he floundered through the ankle-deep mud and picked up two wet and dripping objects not far from each other. As he stood looking at them in consternation, Abna came to his side.

"Vi and Viona's helmets, eh?" Abna took one of them and examined it. "Apparently ripped off, perhaps by the Ajipurs."

"Looks like it. You realize how this affects things? If they are still alive, which no longer seems likely, they are exposed to the Mind. Anything might happen."

"I know. We—"

"Danger!" Marita interrupted quickly. "I can sense it where you can't. The Ajipurs are not far away and heading towards us. We've got to move. They've probably been driven off by the storms."

Abna and Mexone did not hesitate a moment longer. They followed the girl's directions and blundered through the sea of mud away from the center of the clearing. Without mishap they succeeded in gaining the surrounding jungle.

"We're safe enough here," Marita said. "But what we do next I don't quite know. Do you want to continue your search for your wife and daughter?"

"To the end," Abna replied grimly, looking at the muddy helmet in his hand, and then at the one Mexone was carrying. "We've just got to find them."

The girl thought for a moment, then she said: "Fortunately, the track through this jungle leads only in one direction, so if by any chance your wife and daughter escaped they would automatically take it. Come—this way."

She began leading the way again, amidst mountainous ferns and through shoulder-high bushes.

"Doesn't seem too promising," Abna sighed at last. "I begin to think it's hopeless, Marita. Perhaps we—"

"Listen!" the girl interrupted, holding up her hand for silence.

Both Abna and Mexone stopped, unable to detect what was evidently apparent to the girl's more accustomed ears.

"Something moving in the vegetation," she explained, her whole attitude one of intentness. "And I don't think it's an Ajipur, either man or woman. They have a different way of doing things."

Abna looked about him, then gave a start as Mexone abruptly grasped his arm. It was a hard, convulsive movement.

"For heaven's sake—look!" the younger man whispered. "Am I dreaming it or is it really there?"

In that instant Abna saw what had caught Mexone's attention, and he could hardly credit it himself. Two pairs of glaring eyes were fixed on them amidst the undergrowth. That in itself would have been startling enough, but when the eyes were topped by a shock of golden hair in one case, and copper-colored tresses in the other, it became positively fantastic.

"Vi!" Abna cried thankfully.

"Viona!" Mexone exclaimed, almost simultaneously.

Their names being called had not the least effect on the two ragged, superbly muscled women who now came, half crouching, out of the jungle. They advanced slowly, lips drawn back in the snarl of an animal—and suddenly, before Abna or Mexone could protect themselves, the two women sprang and began to fight and claw with tigerish ferocity.

Abruptly Abna grasped the situation.

"Let them have it," he shouted to Mexone, struggling with the crushing, iron strength of the Amazon's arms. "They're demented. No helmets. Knock 'em out."

There was nothing else for it. Abna did not hesitate a moment. He delivered a smashing blow into the Amazon's face, and then another to her jaw. At the second punch she relaxed limply and with a little groan dropped prostrate into the undergrowth, her tattered clothes barely concealing her perfect form.

Mexone glanced at her, dodged the talon-like ripping of Viona's fingernails, and then decided on the same tactics. He waited for his opportunity and then slammed home an uppercut that literally lifted Viona from her feet.

"I never expected to have to treat my wife that way," Mexone panted, smearing the back of his hand over the cuts on his face.

"It isn't Vi and Viona we've been fighting, but mindless, crazy animals," Abna replied quickly. "Get the helmets on their heads and then maybe we'll get some sense into them."

He dived for one of the helmets, which had fallen into the undergrowth and slipped it swiftly over the Amazon's head. In another moment the same treatment had been applied to Viona. Then the two men set to work on reviving the two senseless, blood-streaked women.

"Okay, Vi, take it easy," Abna murmured, as at length the Amazon opened her eyes. "You're safe enough."

The Amazon looked at him for a while with no recognition in her violet eyes, then gradually comprehension seemed to dawn.

"Abna! What's been happening? Where are we?"

"In the jungle on the planet Moyel. You came under the influence of the Wave."

"But you're dead! I remember now. Viona and I left for you dead—"

"We're not dead, or anywhere near it." Abna shook the Amazon gently. "Get a grip on yourself, Vi!"

"I remember now what happened," she said. "And thank goodness you're still alive."

Abna grinned. "Thanks for being so sentimental about it. You couldn't get along properly without me, eh?"

"I can always solve my own problems, Abna," the Amazon replied, shrugging. "But it's always best to have a companion...." She moved over quickly to Viona and for a moment relaxed far enough to pass a gentle hand over the girl's coppery hair. "All right, Viona?" she asked anxiously.

"Yes, I'm all right now." The girl looked shaken as she stood in Mexone's grip. "I'm just beginning to realize what happened. Our helmets went when a flash of lightning struck us, and after that we just—blanked out."

"And became savages," Abna said, coming forward. "But we needn't go into that.… Oh, meet Marita, who has been a very great help to Mexone and me. She did her best to enable us to find you, but we did it accidentally in the end."

"But this Wave doesn't seem to affect you," the Amazon remarked, puzzled, drawing her ripped clothing more discreetly about her.

"She's inured to it," Abna explained. "She is under the influence all the time, but there's a story attached to that which you must hear sometime. Right now I should think the pair of you need food and drink."

"That's easily settled," Marita said quickly, and darted away into the midst of the trees. She was soon back, carrying monstrous clumps of grape-like fruit.

"Quite safe," Abna said, as the Amazon looked dubious. "We've had some. And as for drinking water—just dip one of these big leaves and you'll get all you want."

The Amazon nodded, and for a while she and Viona spent their time attending to the demands of hunger and thirst. When it was over, a troubled look came to the Amazon's face.

"In spite of all we've been through then, Abna, we're no better off?" she asked. "In fact, worse off. We don't even know where the spaceship is?"

"No." Abna gave a grim look at the shattered object on his wrist, which had once been a compass. "The prospect is not too bright."

The Amazon's eyes strayed to Marita, sitting a little distance apart on a shattered tree stump.

"And where do you fit into all this, Marita?" she asked, at which the girl rose and came forward.

"Tell her your story," Abna suggested. "I'll fill in the blanks."

The girl nodded and found another closer tree stump on which to sit. Then she told the same story she had related to Abna, and as he had promised, he interpolated the scientific implications where necessity demanded.

"So that's it," the Amazon said finally, musing.

"The Mind, as you call it, is buried somewhere under the rubble of this city. I am all for continuing the search for the Mind. If only we can find it and destroy it, two worlds will be saved: Falsen, and this planet. Freed from mental slavery, your people, Marita, will soon rise to the scientific heights necessary to overcome these cosmic storms and supply your world with a new magnetic shield. Indeed, we would help you in that."

Marita nodded slowly. "That is true—but where do we find the Mind? How can you locate it?"

"You haven't such a thing as a detector, I suppose? A device for registering thought-waves and their direction? An instrument like that would lead us to the source of the trouble right away."

Marita began to shake her dark head slowly, then suddenly she paused and a new light came into her eyes.

"We—might have," she said hesitantly.

"Might have?" Abna repeated. "How do you mean?"

"Back in my town there are all kinds of scientific treasures saved from the disaster of the storm. Some of the Elders were wise enough to save them and keep them in storage, even though their mentalities had dropped to such a low ebb they were no longer capable of understanding their use. Perhaps you might be able to find such an instrument there?"

Abna rose quickly. "What are we waiting for? Sounds like a distinct possibility to me. Lead the way back, Marita."

Marita obeyed promptly, rather proud of her position as guide to four people so obviously gifted in the arts of science. The journey proved to be a long one, through forest and city ruins as before, and once they were held up for nearly an hour as yet another of the frightful storms raged and blasted the ground and the heavens. Then on again. Until, as the night shut down, they came at last to the torch-lighted region of Marita's town.

"There!" she exclaimed finally. "Take your pick of what you understand. For us, none of the instruments has the slightest meaning."

The quartet did not answer; they were too amazed. For the torchlight was casting on to hundreds and thousands of various instruments, some of them stacked on shelves along the four walls, and others piled into massive baskets on the floor.

"Start searching," Abna said promptly, and while he and the Amazon started on one pair of baskets, Mexone and Viona investigated the shelves.

Progress was slow, because there were so many relics that were of fascinating interest to those so minded. Many of the things the four understood, as common appliances of a scientific laboratory—but others were quite beyond them, products of a science complicated beyond belief.

"I wonder," Abna said presently, "if this thing is what we're looking for?"

He held forth an instrument in a plush case. It looked exactly like some kind of compass, its needle delicately balanced and swinging freely inside what was clearly a vacuum globe.

"May be an ordinary compass," the Amazon said. "Trouble is we have no ordinary compass of our own to check whether that needle is pointing northwards. If it isn't, then it is obviously indicating something else."

Abna glanced up. "Marita, do you know which is the northerly point of the compass?" he asked.

She nodded and pointed. "That way is north."

"Good!" the Amazon exclaimed. "Then this needle is not a compass needle. It may be a thought-wave detector, Abna, insofar as it is on the basic design of the one we created on Falsen. I suggest we try it."

"Would it not be better," Marita suggested, "for you all to rest—even sleep—a while? I, too, am in need of sleep. A few hours can't make much difference."

"She's right," Mexone said. "She hasn't got our staying power for one thing—but even apart from that, a little sleep wouldn't do any of us any harm."

Abna nodded. "All right. We'll start off again at dawn."

* * * * * * *

As they had promised themselves, the five set off again when daylight had returned to the dreary world of Moyel. Marita seemed refreshed from her slumbers, and indeed since falling in with the quartet seemed to have become a brighter and more intelligent girl altogether.

The journey differed but little from the previous trips. As usual, it went through forest and ruins alternately, Marita taking a long detour so as to avoid any possible chance of contacting the regions inhabited by the Ajipurs. Abna carried the compass—or, as he hoped, the detector—and he made constant checks upon it to insure that it was operating correctly.

It was late in the afternoon, according to Marita, who had a good idea of the time on Moyel, when the needle showed a variation. It was commencing to dip slightly downwards on its universal pivot—and the farther the party progressed the more the needle dipped.

"I believe it's working," Abna murmured tensely. "If the Mind machine is buried, and this instrument is indeed a thought detector, then plainly the needle will dip to the vertical. At that moment we'll be directly above the Mind."

His reasoning proved correct. Perhaps an hour later, in the midst of crumbling ruins of stone and metal, the needle was pointing directly downwards to the ground. Obviously, then, they had reached journey's end.

They searched for at least another hour, the light fast commencing to fade, before they happened upon a monstrous cairn of stones. Beyond it, caved in, were smashed stone steps leading downwards.

"Might be it," the Amazon said quickly. "We'd better move fast if we want to find out before the daylight's gone."

She had hardly spoken when the daylight vanished, with its usual abruptness. The party was left in the pitchy darkness, Abna gripping the detector firmly.

"Certainly we're not going to let this interrupt us. Where's your torch, Vi?"

The Amazon felt in her belt—which with its instruments had survived the vicissitudes of their adventures—tugged out the atomic torch and snapped it on. Instantly a brilliant beam shafted into the darkness.

"Forward," Abna said, and headed the party down a narrow passage of crumbled stonework. Then suddenly he halted, the torches blazing on to a solid metal door. It looked to be made of bronze with a mighty handle in the center and no sign whatever of latches. Abna pulled on it with all his strength, but he might as well have tried to pull the planet itself.

"How is it fastened?" the Amazon asked. "What sort of a frame is it in?"

That started a minute investigation, and the pulling away of stonework and rubbish. Finally it could be revealed that the door was sunken into a massive bronze frame, which in turn was imbedded in the stonework. A more solid job could hardly be imagined.

"I don't like the look of it," the Amazon complained. "Whoever sank this door into the bedrock certainly didn't mean it to open. And there must be so much beyond which is worthy of our attention."

"Nothing less than the Mind itself, I imagine," Abna replied; then, after thinking for a moment, he pulled out his proton gun, opened it to the widest flame nozzle, and fired. The hardly visible beam of destruction plainly stuck the door, but it made not the least impression save for a discoloration of the metal.

"We've small bombs for use in a real emergency," Viona put in. "Why not try one?"

The others nodded silent agreement, at which Viona withdrew one of the bombs from her instrument belt, set the time-mechanism in operation, and then hastily motioned to the steps. As fast as they could go the five blundered up to the safety above and waited for results.

They were not long in happening. The bomb, small though it was, exploded with devastating force. Earth and rock came shooting up the steps from the blast, and over the site of the door the ground took a sudden leap skywards. When the dust and smoke had cleared, the mighty door was visible at the bottom of a huge crater—but the door was undisturbed in the bedrock. The force of the bomb had not even scratched it.

"I wonder...." The Amazon spoke musingly. "I just wonder if it would work?"

She didn't explain herself there and then, but instead surveyed the immense open crater in which the door lay. It was noteworthy that no point beyond the door had been blasted either. The landscape was solid—which indicated some immensely hard underground covering protecting whatever lay beyond the door.

"Wonder if what would work?" Abna asked.

"Lightning! The one thing on this world that has devastating power, far more than any we can ever achieve. If we can direct it on to that door, we might stand a chance. Natural electricity of such tremendous voltage might do the trick."

"Very possibly, but there's the trifling matter of directing the lightning to the desired spot. What do you propose to do? Talk to it nicely?"

The Amazon smiled faintly. "I do believe you're annoyed, Abna, because I've thought one better than you for once. I wouldn't have suggested the idea without having the means handy. It comes to this: when Viona and I were captured by the pygmies, we were tied to posts that were made of copper. They stood about fifty feet high and most certainly they were irresistible attractors of electricity."

Abna's expression changed. "You mean get one of them, put it in contact with the door, and— Well, let nature takes its course?"

"Exactly! And I don't see why it shouldn't work, either. The only trouble will be dealing with those confounded pygmies again."

"There won't be any trouble about that," Mexone put in grimly. "Last we saw of their area it had been smashed flat in the latest storm. The hardest job of all will be to uproot one of those fifty-foot copper columns. They must be sunk a good way down. Still, the united strength of the four of us might do it. Myself, I'm all for the idea."

Since Viona did not raise any objections either, the plan was decided upon, and to Marita there again fell the task of being the guide through the jungle at night.

* * * * * *

None of the pygmies was in sight amidst the drying, sticky mud. Presumably they had chosen other quarters after the violence of the storm that destroyed their habitat—but the copper posts were still there, pointing to the gray and swirling sky.

"Yes, Mexone and I saw them before," Abna commented, "but we didn't bother to look at close quarters."

He strode across the mud and, reaching the first post, examined it carefully. Then with the muzzle of his gun he scraped away at the surface, and produced the bright, coppery gleam that could only come from the pure metal.

"Certainly copper—and pure at that," he announced. "Now let's see what we can do."

Immediately they all moved into position, one behind the other. Abna waited until they were all braced, their feet in the firmest position they could find in the mud. Then he nodded.

"All right—heave!" he instructed. "Heave!"

Their united force had a result. The pillar began to tilt sideways—farther and farther—until at last it fell gradually to the horizontal, uprooting the ground around its base as it went.

CHAPTER EIGHT
THE SUPER COMPUTER

"Good!" Abna exclaimed, breathing hard. "We've done it!" He stood looking in satisfaction on the twenty feet or so of extra length that had been uprooted—making a seventy-foot pillar of copper in all.

"That's all we need," the Amazon said, likewise surveying. "The best conductor of lightning ever made. The sooner we transport it back to that door, the better."

They paused only long enough to get their breath back after their labors, then they began the task of hauling the copper pillar on to their shoulders. Marita was too small to take part—and in any case she was to be their guide. Supplied with the detector that Abna had formerly carried, she led the way as the heavy burden was borne along.

The actual arranging of the post was not difficult. The Amazon herself directed operations, as well as doing most of the hard work. To plant the post was not nearly such a tough task as carrying it through the jungle. It was only sunk to a depth of two feet, after which its own weight bedded it down. It lay at an angle, flush with the door, its topmost point rearing up in a solitary splendor.

"That's that," the Amazon said finally. "For the first time we really want a storm, which is probably a good reason why there won't be one for a long time."

But in that assumption she was wrong. About two hours later, when the five were resting from their exertions and enjoying some of the inevitable fruits for nourishment, there stole a darkness over the face of things. The Amazon glanced up quickly.

"Here we go," she commented briefly. "And we'd better find shelter. Looks as though this one's going to be a good one."

Suddenly, with the blinding abruptness that characterized all things on this strange planet, the storm broke. Lightning waterfalled down the sky some distance away, and the ground smoked and heaved where it struck. Thunder rolled and detonated, but the distance was still considerable. But not for long. In the space of seconds the fury built up to maximum as the heavens fully discharged their load.

Yet another flash came, and even another, the ground shaking almost incessantly now under the unimaginable din. The five winced at the noise and shut their eyes to the incessant dazzle—until they suddenly realized there wasn't anything anymore. As usual, the storm had gone as though it had never been, leaving a quagmire of mud and newly created lakes.

"I couldn't exactly see what happened, but I believe we've done it!" Abna exclaimed. "The rain hid the view—"

He scrambled quickly to his feet and slopped through the mud to the edge of the crater, the others coming after him. In the growing light of the after-storm they gazed in delight upon the vision they had hoped to see.

The pillar was gone—that they had known—but the mighty door had also been partially fused into molten metal. Not all of it had been destroyed—even by that terrific flash of lightning—but enough had been melted away to make ingress a possibility.

"This is it!" Abna cried exultantly. "At last!"

He raced down the slope with the others behind him and at last arrived, mud-splashed and panting, at the gap in the door. Beyond the gap was a funereal darkness. One by one they each peered into it and then looked at one another questioningly.

"All right, we go ahead," the Amazon said. "We didn't go through all that just to gaze into a hole of darkness. I'm all for risking it." She tugged out her torch and flashed a brilliant beam into the gap, which revealed a portion of obviously man-made metal tunnel perfectly dry. "Here we go."

They reached the end of the tunnel without mishap, to find two others branching at right angles. It was a matter of deciding which one to take.

"We'll try left first," Abna said. "No use us separating. We don't know what we might run into."

Accordingly he set the example; but he had hardly gone a dozen yards before he started abruptly before a sudden flood of light. It penetrated into every quarter of the tunnel, making the torches superfluous. For a moment or two the five stopped, impressed by the sudden wonder of this happening.

"Photo-electric cell or something," the Amazon said. "It must have actuated a light switch when we crossed the beam—or rather when you did, Abna."

He nodded and went on again. As it happened, the tunnel did not proceed for any great distance. It abruptly took a sharp-angled turn and finished in three small steps. Abna stood at the top of them, even his breath taken away for a moment by the incredible sight that had unfolded. In the course of his adventures he had seen many scientific laboratories, devoted to all kinds of purposes, but never one the like of this. It was almost unbelievable.

In area it covered perhaps three square miles, so much so that the farthermost walls were lost in distance. Everything was bathed in the pearly radiance of indirect lighting, and seemed to have been designed after the fashion of a wheel. The 'spokes' were great banks of machines, linked on the 'rim' of the wheel to multiple switchboards.

Between each 'spoke' ran an aisleway—while the central 'hub' contained one gigantic machine, fifty feet high by thirty feet broad, a great monster of a thing sprouting cables, lenses, and shining panels and mechanisms. Somehow, each one instinctively knew that this was the thing they sought…the Mind.

"You belong to a very clever race, Marita," Abna said presently, turning to her. "Far cleverer than any I have ever known.

"I know," she answered, in simple acceptance of the fact. "If only such glory could be reached again, what a happy day that would be."

"And there," the Amazon said musingly, "is the monster which has wrecked your genius and brings tumult to two worlds."

She strode off down the aisleway and Abna followed her at a more leisurely pace: Viona, Mexone, and Marita took their time, staring at the monstrous engines of science as they went. So at length the Amazon reached the Mind, the root cause of all their troubles. She stood surveying it speculatively, her eyes wandering over the maze of wires and up towards the lighted displays that showed the giant was working. Then she peered at the metal of which the thing was made. It was of a texture she had never encountered before, possessing a bronze tint, but was not actually bronze itself.

"Certainly is a magnificent feat of engineering," Abna said, coming up. "And from the look of it it's pretty indestructible. I'll gamble that metal's tougher even than the door with which we had such trouble."

"Maybe, but this is a different proposition entirely. There are wires to this thing—arteries that supply the lifeblood, so to speak. And there's no doubt the thing is functioning."

"No doubt whatever," Abna agreed. "From the look of things it is absorbing its power from those generators over there. What they in turn connect to I haven't the slightest idea."

"Probably cosmic energy. Nothing else would keep this thing going constantly at a steady and unvarying level."

Marita, who had been listening to this high-flown scientific conversation in silence, ventured a comment.

"There have been times in the past when our scientists have spoken of special intelligence," she said

The Amazon glanced at her. "Then that explains a good deal. Even for intelligence, existing as ethereal waves, there is a byproduct so to speak. Dregs. It is probably the dregs of intelligence that this unspeakable monstrosity picks up and re-radiates. Hardly anything else could account for the vileness of the conceptions it creates."

With that she turned and took her proton gun into her hand. She sighted it at a tempting maze of wires and pressed the button. The usual hardly visible fan of energy blasted forth—but nothing happened. The wires remained unharmed despite the onslaught.

"That's queer," she muttered, frowning, and Abna gave a faint smile.

"Is it? You can be sure that the scientists will have made these wires, and their coverings, of the most indestructible materials known to them. And that's saying a good deal."

"Well, there must be a vulnerable part somewhere," the Amazon snapped, irritated at her failure, and forthwith she began to prowl around the machine, surveying it from various angles. Time and again she flashed her deadly protonic gun, but without result. There was not the slightest effect from it. Finally, even she was compelled to admit defeat.

"If this gun won't do it, perhaps a mini A-bomb will," she said, feeling in her instrument belt. "Worth a try, do you think?"

"Yes, maybe," Abna agreed, a trifle dubiously.

The others said nothing, for at that moment the Amazon pulled the pin from the A-bomb, and then raced at top speed down the aisleway to what she judged was a safe distance. The explosion, when it came, was tremendous in the confined space—confined, that is, compared to the outdoors.

There was a brilliant flash of flame, a report that stunned the eardrums, then the familiar curling mushroom of acrid, radioactive smoke. Slowly, it began to disperse.

The Mind machine was untouched. Not even scratched, and its panel displays were glowing as brightly as before. Nor, apparently, had any other machines suffered from the effects of the blast.

Abna whistled as he straightened up. "That certainly is some metal! Wonder what it's made of?"

The Amazon was looking annoyed. "This is positively fantastic! The enemy within our grasp and we can't do anything to destroy it!"

"Something will occur to us presently," Abna said, with a patient smile. "In the meantime, suppose we see what these other machines do? One of them might even be able to help us in the matter of destruction."

One machine in particular was quite intriguing. It

was, so Viona discovered, a food machine. By pressing various buttons it was possible, after a little practice, to produce almost any meal, hot or cold, from synthetic materials. In the end, after about an hour of experiment, Viona had succeeded in producing quite an Earthly dinner, complete with hot drinks.

* * * * * *

The machines were so incredibly complicated that the visitors' scientific skills were at a loss. The race who had populated their planet before they had been eclipsed had undoubtedly been surpassingly clever, and doubtless most of their works were brilliant, could they only have been understood.

Finally, it was the Amazon who came upon an instrument that made sense. Studying it, she finally came to the conclusion that the object was a super-computer—some kind of electronic brain, but far advanced beyond normal Earth standards.

"What do you make of it?" she asked, calling Abna over. "Is it a mathematical machine, or not?"

"No doubt of it," he responded, pondering its lines and the many dials and keys. "Take a bit of time to work out what makes it tick, though. Don't forget that mathematics seem to be different in this System to what we're accustomed to."

"I know—but I think this machine is worth the undivided contemplation of all of us. It might find a way by mathematics to destroy the Mind—even return us to our own space."

"Agreed," Abna nodded. "All right, we'll go to work on it."

By and large the five forgot all about the outer world: they were too interested in the scientific wonderland. They even forgot about the storms that were probably raging at intervals beyond their sight and hearing. They ate, slept, and concentrated—even Marita, though she took no active part in trying to analyze the mathematical machine. She preferred to help Viona with perfecting the mysteries of the food-instrument and helping to prepare meals as and when they were required.

"From the look of things," Abna said, after nearly a week of study, "the various machines in here are all slaves of either the Mind, or the mathematical machine. The arrangement of wires seems to suggest that. It looks to me as though the mathematical machine is connected to other devices, which in turn respond when required. I should think that by now we know enough to give the machine a test. Incredible though it seems, it is so sensitive that even speaking to it and making a request is sufficient to set it in action."

"These people certainly knew their science," Viona said, with an admiring shake of the head. "How's chances for thinking up something to destroy the Mind?"

"We're going to try that as soon as we've finished this meal," the Amazon replied. "It all depends if the basic figures for such a conception even exist. Probably they don't."

And, immediately after the meal was over, the Amazon, Abna, and Mexone set about their first experiment with the machine. They knew, from the preliminary rehearsals, what they were going to do—and did it. They were rewarded by seeing the machine's display panels light up. After that it proceeded to whir gently.

"Think it's right?" Mexone asked anxiously.

The Amazon shrugged. "If it isn't, it simply won't work. We will have to hope for the best. We know what we've asked for—a formula for the destruction of the Mind. Have to see what happens."

So they stood and watched the mathematical monster as it went to work. They expected it to take a long time, but rather to their surprise it finished its calculations within ten minutes. A monitor screen displayed a single mathematical symbol, which Marita interpreted as 'zero.'

"Might have known it," Abna sighed. "Zero computation—which is another way of saying there's nothing doing. Well, anyway, we've found the way to make the thing work. Have to devise some other means, I suppose."

CHAPTER NINE
FLIGHT OF DESTRUCTION

"Oh, this is intolerable!" the Amazon declared angrily, much later. "All this stuff around us, every resource of science, and we can't find a way to defeat the Mind! What kind of fools are we?"

"We're not fools," Abna told her quietly. "In fact, I'm inclined to think we've been very ingenious so far.... And I'm not so sure that we're done even yet. First, let's consider our advantages. The Mind cannot know what we're thinking about because of these helmets. Right?"

"What of it?" the Amazon asked impatiently.

"This! We can discuss plans without it knowing what we're up to." Abna grinned suddenly as though his thoughts pleased him. "I think, with the aid of our mathematical baby here, that we ought to build *Ultra III*, a new version of our former cruiser of the void."

"Well, that's quite a good idea," the Amazon admitted, rather surprised, "but hadn't we better keep to the matter on hand? How do we destroy the Mind machine?"

"With the *Ultra III*. There's no other way."

"I'll admit it will have deadly weapons on it," the Amazon said. "Every known offensive weapon of science, in fact, but that still doesn't make us any better off. This Mind machine is proof against all things like that."

Abna became serious. "It is not proof against an object with large mass traveling at almost the speed of light. My idea is this: build the *Ultra III*, which we need anyway, and we have plenty of room in this laboratory to do it. Once that's done we'll force a way out of here—"

"How?" Viona asked pointedly. "As far as we know, the walls and ceiling are as thick and impregnable as that door which gave us so much trouble."

"No doubt of it, but by the time we've finished, the *Ultra* will have everything necessary to penetrate that kind of stuff. Don't forget we take our weapon power from the atomic plant, and that will surely blast us a way through the ceiling to the open above. That will expose the Mind machine to the open as well."

"Then?" the Amazon asked, frowning.

"Then we pinpoint the exact position of the Mind machine. We have it worked out to the last fraction. Following that, we take the *Ultra* into space for a distance of perhaps a million miles, before turning round for the return journey. Then we pile on the acceleration as we head back to this planet—we'll still be in free space so no friction can develop—until we have gained almost the speed of light. Once that is achieved, we flash down to our pinpointed target and up again to space. On the downward sweep we'll drive straight into the Mind machine. It will all happen so fast it won't have time to devise the necessary precautions to save itself. It will be instantly vaporized by the terrible force of the collision."

"But hitting the atmosphere at that kind of speed will be like striking a solid object," Mexone pointed out. "It will generate a terrific amount kinetic energy before we even reach the surface—"

"We'll be moving so fast it won't have time to incinerate the ship, and in any case, the *Ultra* will be encased by a force screen which will protect us. The atmosphere is only composed of gas, don't forget— the effect will be like diving through water. The *real* impact will be when we reach the surface and strike the Mind machine itself. The energy released by the huge mass of the *Ultra* traveling at almost the speed of light and striking a solid object will utterly destroy the Mind!"

As the Amazon was still pondering, Abna added: "It's that or nothing. We've tried everything else."

That settled the Amazon. "All right, we'll try it. If it fails, we'll fail with it, so it's neck or nothing. We'd better get busy drafting out the basic mathematics for the building of the *Ultra III*. It'll be a pretty long job."

* * * * * * *

The Amazon had not exaggerated when she had said it would be a long job to build the *Ultra III*. The mountains of complexity that had to be waded through at times got her neck-deep in problems, but as usual Abna stepped in with a suggestion or correction, which smoothed out the difficulty—and so the basic formula began to take shape. This was definitely a job between Abna and the Amazon alone. They had built the mighty *Ultra II* in the first place, each providing their own modifications and improvements, so again it had to be both of them who did the designing. So much so that the *Ultra III* promised to be far superior even to its marvelous predecessor, both in the matter of armament, comfort, and speed. The power plant, for instance, was twice its original size, and capable of developing an almost unheard of release of atomic energy from a small core of basic copper.

The first thing that had to be done was to create a team of robots who could undertake the initial construction. This was a simple matter, and since the orders were straightforward enough and not directed against the Mind, there was no undue influence to stop them doing exactly as they were told. With their aid, the skeleton foundation of the *Ultra III* began to take shape. Everything necessary was provided by the slave machines, all of which provided their offerings by atomic transmutation, creating their materials from the elements of the atmosphere itself. How it was done was a source of never-ending wonder and mystery.

The surprising thing was, that when the outer plates came to be fitted into position, they were not as specified in the original calculation. They came out as a slightly bronzy metal with an inconceivable hardness.

"All the better," Abna shrugged, when tests had been made. "This stuff is the same as the door—so hard nothing ordinary can make the least impression. With a four-foot-thick wall of that forming the basic shell of the *Ultra*—and augmented by a force screen—we'll be impregnable."

A month passed and the exterior of the mighty machine was finished. It measured 500 feet in length by 100 in width at its widest part. Tail and nose both tapered to a point. Then began the real job of constructing the power plant and control panels with all their wealth of intricacy. It took the combined brains of Abna and the Amazon, and every moment of their waking hours, to construct the necessary set-up, and even then it took them six weeks of grinding toil before they pronounced themselves satisfied.

Radio, television, radar, x-ray, and electronic devices by the score followed One room alone was entirely fitted with computing equipment, intended to detect the slightest flaw in the running of the super-scientific machine.

"And now," the Amazon said, surveying the enormous, bronzy length, "comes the greatest test of all. I must say that I feel more confident, Abna, since we have a shell of this new metal. It is unbreakable by any conventional means, so it ought to prove strong enough when we have to smash our way out of this underground cavern."

Her eyes strayed to the baleful Mind machine, some distance away from the *Ultra*. A sudden thought seemed to strike her.

"The sooner we get on with the job, the better. Poor Thorard on Falsen must be thinking by now that we are never going to return. What about provisioning the ship?"

"Unnecessary," Abna replied. "After the deed we shall descend to see if we've managed it. Then, if we have, we'll load up for departure. If anything happens...." His lips tightened. "Well, if anything happens we shan't need anything."

"How about you, Marita?" the Amazon asked the girl. "This chance we're taking may not come off. It is not fair to take you with us when death may result. Perhaps you'd better—"

"I'm coming with you," she said, without hesitation. "I can hardly imagine my life without you anymore. You are such fantastically wonderful people."

"We'll need to be this time," Abna smiled. "All right—the decision is your own. Let's go."

With that he turned, passed through the airlock, and entered the control room of the machine. In silence the others followed him, then the airlock switch closed. It shut with such tightness and such perfection that there was no trace of where it joined to the main frame. On top of that two sheaths of hermetically sealing rubber slid into place and anchored themselves.

"Here we go," Abna murmured. "One of you take over the disintegrator guns. That'll make our path easier."

The Amazon moved promptly and, with the switches,

angled the guns to the required position, directly facing the roof. She sat looking into the oblique mirrors that gave her a perfect view of what was transpiring.

Abna nodded to himself, glanced once more over the controls, and then applied the smallest level of power. Immediately the countless tons of the *Ultra III* began to rise effortlessly, emitting only the faintest wisp of smoke from the exhaust fins.

"Right!" Abna said briefly. "The guns, Vi."

Instantly they blasted forth, but they made no effect on the roof of the laboratory. Obviously the metal was proof against anything man-made in the way of energy, but not against the shattering force of a direct lightning flash.

"It hasn't broken the ceiling but I'll wager it's softened it up," Abna said tensely. "Here's where we find out."

He kept the controls on the same power-level and inevitably the great mass of the *Ultra* finally hit the ceiling of the vast cavern. Just for an instant the power plant shrieked furiously against an immovable barrier, then monstrous fissures and cracks appeared in the ceiling as the irresistible pressure continued. Abna grinned and increased the power.

That did it! The ceiling shattered abruptly and revealed a mass of bedrock above. Like a tank plowing through mud the *Ultra* crushed its way through the rocks, leaving behind it an avalanche that tumbled down into the laboratory. Within a few minutes it was free of the barrier, and with a sudden jerk gained the outer air. It was daylight. The same gray, drab light that lay eternally over this world of Moyel.

"That's certainly some crater down there!" Mexone exclaimed as he, Viona, and Marita crowded around the window. "Looks as if we smashed the entire laboratory ceiling to bits, Abna."

"All the better," he responded, grinning—then locking the controls so that the *Ultra* floated motionless 100 feet above the smashed laboratory, he added: "Here's where we do some precise mathematics. We've got to pinpoint the position of that Mind machine in our computers so that we know where it is—and also take account of the planet's rotation and orbital speed. When we really pick up speed, and beyond the atmosphere at that, we shan't be able to see it because of our velocity. It will all be done by instruments. Let's get busy."

This was a task that needed all the mathematical skill of the quartet. But little by little the problem was worked out, the final computations being worked out in space, from a low orbit of the planet. The four dials that were to give the exact reading were set at zero.

"Right," Abna said in satisfaction, giving a final check-over of the instruments. "We've got all the readings we need. I'll take the controls, and set them in gear with the computer readings. Vi, you stand by to create the force screen around the ship to protect us at the point of impact. Our inertia nullifiers should enable us to remain conscious even near the speed of light. You others had better lie down—especially you, Marita—

otherwise you'll never be able to stand it. Now, are we ready?"

"Carry on," Viona said, settling into position.

Abna applied the power steadily. Marita was the only one who gave an exclamation as the mighty cruiser moved skywards at an angle of forty-five degrees. The control cabin remained on a level keel, of course, thanks to the gyroscopic controls. The *Ultra* sped away from Moyel, then began to turn in a vast arc through space, until its prow was realigned with the planet, now more than a million miles distant.

Abna increased the power relentlessly, and each time the *Ultra* responded by a sudden jerk as it increased its acceleration. Marita gasped at the bewildering speed.

Faster, and still ever faster. The stars began to blur with the gathering speed. They were no longer fixed points by which to register velocity. Marita lay in breathless awe, her startled eyes staring at the mirror reflecting the planet below. It was no longer a small point of light in space, but a visibly expanding globe of gray-white, so rapidly was the *Ultra* hurtling towards it.

Presently, with the mounting whine of the power plant, the velocity of 93,000 miles a second had been reached—exactly half the speed of light. Abna gave a quick glance at the instrument readings. Everything was in order.

"I've activated the force screen around us," the Amazon said. "You three all right? She added shortly, glancing around from her control panel.

"Perfectly," Viona responded calmly. "When do you start to really move, Dad?"

"Move!" Marita gasped, dazed. "It is beyond me how anything can even travel as fast as this."

"We'll go a lot faster yet," Abna told her. "From now on until maximum you'll certainly feel the strain. We all will."

How right he was became evident soon as the vessel still continued to accelerate at breathtaking speed. Faster and ever faster.

"We've got sufficient velocity," Abna said curtly. "Direction fixed."

"Now," the Amazon said. "Let her go."

Down the *Ultra* went, atmosphere screaming and crashing behind it in multiple thunder as it ripped through layer after layer at a speed beyond imagination. In the space of a fraction of a second from entering the atmosphere it reached its target. There was a violent shudder through the ship, which had hardly gone before the *Ultra* was out in space again, its upward climb completed. Abna released a little sigh and kept the vessel going upwards, though he cut the accelerative power down to zero.

"As far as I can tell," he said, "the job is done. That brief shudder we felt should have been the *Ultra* crashing into the Mind machine. When the speed has been sufficiently reduced, we'll go back and find out."

Reduction in speed, however, proved to be no simple matter. It was a full two hours before the vessel showed sign of really slowing down, and by this time it was several million miles from Moyel, leaving the planet behind as a tiny gray-wide globe.

Only at this point could Abna begin to realign the vessel—and so at length, by describing an enormous arc in the void, the *Ultra* was on its way back, at a relatively slow acceleration.

By the time it reached Moyel's crazy atmosphere, evening was settling. There was also one violent electrical storm through the midst of which they sailed invincibly; so at last they came over the spot where the laboratory had been, and hardly dared to look if their experiment had been a success.

"Yes, we did it!" Mexone cried in triumph, staring through the port. "Smashed it to blazes! Take a look!"

This was exactly what Abna, the Amazon, Viona, and Mexone were doing, their eyes gleaming with satisfaction at the sight of the once-impregnable Mind machine. To say it had been utterly and completely destroyed was an understatement.

Nothing remained of that incredibly violent collision except a scattering of fused metallic parts. The rest had been smashed into absolute dust. Yet, so flawlessly had the impact been timed, no other machines had suffered damage. Being already sufficiently proofed against the tremendous heat and blast wave that had been released, they still stood unharmed, though, of course, without any laboratory roof. The fallen rocks created by their vessel's departure had been vaporized.

"Well, that's that," Abna grinned. "The Mind is no more. The people of Falsen can breathe freely again, and your folks, Marita, can start to rebuild."

"And there's no longer any need of these confounded things," the Amazon exclaimed, unbuckling and then wrenching off her helmet.

Abna did not trouble to remove his own helmet until he had brought the *Ultra* down close to the ruined laboratory. Then he opened the airlock and stepped outside. It gave him a great sense of personal satisfaction to move toward the spot where the Mind had been and remove his helmet at the same time. Now, at close quarters, it was plain to see that the baleful machine had been literally torn out of its rock foundations by the impact of the *Ultra* and utterly destroyed.

"Thank you, my dear friends—thank you," Marita said seriously, coming up and grasping the hands of both Abna and the Amazon. "You don't know what this means to our people."

"I think we do," the Amazon responded. "It's entirely up to you now, Marita. We must return to Falsen and report to them that the Mind is no more. Then we must work out a means of getting back to our own time and space. We've done all here that we came for."

"I shall never forget you," the girl of Moyel said, with a breathless earnestness. "Already I can feel my mind beginning to function as it used to. There is not that deadening weight upon it. No longer a sense of constriction."

"So be it then." Abna smiled. "Best of luck, Marita, and it has been great fun knowing you."

"You will none of you ever come back?" Marita

asked anxiously, as they turned back toward the *Ultra*.

The Amazon shook her head. "Not as far as we know, Marita. We have other jobs to do, in our own space far from here— Just remember that the Cosmic Crusaders gave you back your civilization. It is up to you to work out how to still the magnetic storms."

The girl nodded slowly and watched the four as they returned to their vessel. The airlock closed. Abna moved to the control board and hesitated for a moment, looking at the lone figure waving a farewell in the fast-approaching night.

CHAPTER TEN
HELL LET LOOSE

The journey to Falsen was but a brief one, accomplished in far shorter time than the outward trip, thanks to the tremendous power of the *Ultra*. Evidently the arrival had been sighted, for when they landed in the grounds surrounding the main laboratories, Thorard and a group of the senior scientists were already waiting.

The moment the airlock opened Thorard came forward with hand extended, and a welcoming smile. "A pleasure to see you again, my friends. We had begun to fear that some disaster had overtaken you."

"It nearly did—quite a few times," Abna responded. "However, we got the upper hand eventually, even to the extent of providing ourselves with a new space machine."

"So I observe." The bald scientist's eyes traveled in brief wonder along the *Ultra*'s immense, bronzy length. "And what of the Wave? We had one other onslaught while you were away, so I assume you were not successful?"

"The Wave will never trouble you again, Thorard. It

is completely destroyed, and it took all our ingenuity to do it."

The scientist's emotion was obvious. "My friends, this is indeed good hearing. What a wonderful thing you have done for us."

"And the people of Moyel," the Amazon added. "They have had—and will have again—a mighty civilization now that menace has been destroyed."

Thorard looked surprised. "Then Moyel is inhabited?"

"By a race supremely above yours," Abna said quietly. "You will do well to establish friendly relations with them and live in peace. Before we leave, we will hand to you the secret of space travel, then you will have no difficulty in contacting them."

"There is no limit to your generosity," the scientist murmured. "But come, my friends, and have a meal. You will certainly be in need of refreshment."

Abna nodded, locked the *Ultra*'s controls, and then led the way at the head of the quartet to the former great room in the administration building, where Thorard had his headquarters. The other scientists, eager to hear the details, came, too.

Then, while the meal progressed, Abna gave every fact, with embellishments from the Amazon.

"Indeed that was a task which demanded superbeings," Thorard commented at length when he and his colleagues had discussed the various aspects.

"To congratulate you seems absurd. All we can do is offer our profound thanks for the release of our people from bondage...." He pondered for a moment, then: "There must be something we can do in return. Some action we can perform to translate our gratitude into action."

"Yes, there is one thing," Abna admitted. "We have simply got to find a way back into our own space. Perhaps we could eventually, but the mathematics here are so different from our own. You are an intelligent race: suppose we gave you the exact details of how we came into this macro-universe, and then left it with you to work out how to reverse the process and return us to our own space?"

"It will take time, Abna," Thorard said finally, "but I see no reason why we can't devise something. The greatest difficulty will lie in transcribing your mathematics into ours. But that is not insurmountable."

Abna shrugged. "The time taken does not signify. In the interval we can take a rest, which we need after our hectic time on Moyel. It will also give us time in which to study your science at our leisure, and answer any questions which may puzzle you."

* * * * * * *

As it happened, however, events began to take a new turn as the days passed in calm tranquility.

It began in the simplest way, and apparently did not mean anything. It appeared that a woman had been attacked on one of the pedestrian streets by an object that was indescribable. Black in color, she had said, shaped rather like an Earthly bat, with a small, vicious head and razed-edged teeth. There was little doubt that the woman had been badly bitten. What made it more serious was that in the space of an hour she was dead, which suggested the bites she had received had been venomous—but how much of her story was true, and how much imagination, was open to question. She had been attacked by something, but there were no witnesses, and an object such as she had described was unknown upon Falsen. All destructive life had been obliterated long ago.

Thorard, as chief scientist, was naturally consulted, but the problem defeated him, and came at a time when he was deep in experiments to repeat Abna's bomb. So he contacted the quartet to see if they had suggestions to offer.

"There has never been anything like it before," Thorard said worriedly. "For that matter, we haven't any bird life at all. It became extinct centuries ago. Yet from all accounts these objects resemble birds, though they are infinitely faster. And I need hardly add that they are deadly poisonous. Have you, with your wider range of knowledge, any conception of what they can be?"

"None at all," the Amazon said, thinking. "We would try to analyze the things if we could be sure where they would strike next. Being in ignorance of that, there isn't much we can do."

"No, I suppose there isn't.... It's all very distracting, particularly at this stage of our experiments. All I can ask is that you will keep a sharp lookout for these things, and if by any chance you spot any, do what you think best."

"Willingly," Abna said. "But any opportunity we have will be by pure chance."

The next day, however, the 'pure chance' arrived—and with it the Deluge. The quartet, for their part, had decided upon a visit to the other side of the planet—purely for reasons of interest and nothing more—and were just outside the airlock of the *Ultra* when the Deluge came.

Their first awareness of it was in a mysterious darkening of the daylight. It was as though evening were coming before its time. Puzzled, the four looked around them—first out toward the city proper where lights were springing up to mitigate the gloom. Then they looked skywards, and stood amazed.

Before the quartet had fully grasped what it was all about the air began to hum, caused by the speed with which the creatures moved through the atmosphere. They descended in a mighty power dive toward the center of the city and the sky magically cleared and lighted. But in the heart of the metropolis, hell was let loose.

In every conceivable place the creatures landed. On buildings, people, vehicles, runways, pedestrian tracks, bridges. They flew through glass at bullet-like velocity. Some even crashed through solid walls without apparent hurt to themselves. Men, women, and children—these latter on their way to the educational centers—were mown down and slaughtered before they even had the opportunity to defend themselves or find out what it was all about.

The quartet outside the *Ultra* saw the main swoop of the creatures and then looked at each other grimly.

"Flying horrors of some sort," the Amazon said curtly. "In the *Ultra* we can outfly them. Let's go."

She led the way into the machine, the others behind her. The airlock was swiftly closed, and Abna sprang to the control board. The moment he moved the power lever the vast machine leaped into the air and shot toward the center of the metropolis. Here the mighty vessel hovered, and in horrified amazement the four looked down on the carnage. From their viewpoint it seemed as though the whole center of the city was being eaten away. No, it was not that. The 'things' were not consuming anything. There were so many of them that they had formed a literal carpet over every-thing, animate and inanimate. Here and there people were running for their lives, but were usually struck down long before they reached safety.

"What in creation are they?" Abna demanded, staring fixedly. "I never saw anything like them before—"

He stopped speaking suddenly and clapped a hand to his forehead. In spite of himself he swayed dizzily before a tremendous mental wave. Obviously it affected the Amazon, Viona, and Mexone at the same time, for it was only with difficulty that they managed to remain standing.

"They're—mental assassins," the Amazon gasped out. "Venom in their physical nature, and killers in their mental makeup; never—never been anything like them before."

She slid to the floor, overcome, and at the same moment Mexone and Viona collapsed, too.

Abna looked around him dazedly. He was still on his feet, fighting with every vestige of his magnificent mind to hold on to his senses—and to a certain extent succeeded, probably because the horrors were not concentrating directly upon him.

At the same time a murderous rage against these invaders consumed him, a natural fury that they should have the effrontery to decimate a peaceful people.

In this mood he staggered to the control board, kept a steel grip on his tortured mind, and grasped the controls. Then he thought better of the situation and instead turned to where the powerful disintegrator gun stood against the farther wall.

He reeled into the saddle in front of it, sighted it by means of the reflecting mirrors—then pressed the button. Instantly, invisible fire commenced to pour on the packed masses of creatures below.

Some of them were decimated instantly. The others took fright and flocked in their tens of thousands to the upper heights.

Upon Abna the mental stranglehold began to lessen. It beat now in irregular waves as the creatures were obviously too disturbed to maintain any regular thought-transmission. He grinned harshly to himself and swept the beam again, wiping out scores of the creatures as they shot upward.

It was at this moment that Abna had the chance to notice an extraordinary thing. The creatures did not fly, as one would have expected them to do. Using some unknown motive force of their own, they simply went upwards, using either some unknown magnetism or invisible means of propulsion.

Abna watched them go—all of them now in a driving cloud—and the mental grip loosened still more.

Suddenly Abna moved—and quickly. He scrambled from the gun saddle, reached the controls, and put on the power. Instantly the *Ultra* began to move upwards with ever-increasing speed, keeping to the rear of the 'birds' and following them to wherever their lair might be. Abna's astonishment grew with the moments. Surely it was not possible that the things lived in outer space?

Yet, amazingly enough, this was the right answer. Without pause the hordes shot beyond the limits of the atmosphere, and with never a pause went forging into the deeps of the void. For a time Abna pursued them, then he shut off the acceleration, slowed down, and gradually returned to Falsen.

By the time he had again come over the metropolis, the Amazon, Viona, and Mexone were completely recovered. They listened to the tale Abna had to tell with mixed feelings.

"What do you imagine they are?" the Amazon demanded. "I never heard of anything like them before."

"They're extremely strong mentally," Abna mused,

"and they certainly are entirely evil in their physical makeup, even as you surmised before you passed out. I'm going to have a closer look at one of them before passing any opinion. There must be dozens of maimed and dead ones down there."

He nodded down toward the city. People had reappeared now and were endeavoring to bring some kind of order out of the chaos the creatures had caused. Abna moved to the control board and slowly lowered the *Ultra* until at length it was settled on a clear space only a few yards from where the worst of the attack had been centered.

There was no difficulty in finding a specimen for examination. It was complete, though dead, and Abna looked at it curiously as it was handed to him.

More than ever was its bat-like appearance noticeable, but it struck him—and the Amazon, Viona, and Mexone, too—that he had never in his experience seen anything that looked so utterly evil. The eyes, though dead, were similar to those of an eagle or vulture, and even in death were pitiless in their inhuman stare. The mouth was a terrible affair resembling a vice, and armed with triple rows of needle-pointed teeth. Altogether, the most frightful creature, for its size, the Crusaders had ever seen.

"Right, this will do," Abna said at length, and returned to the *Ultra* with the other behind him. Then he wasted no time in hurtling back to Thorard's domain.

The scientist was obviously distressed by the happenings in the city, which had, of course, been immediately reported to him. Then he looked at the dead creature that Abna was holding in one hand, rather like something he had brought from a market.

"Tell me, Abna, do you think a further attack is possible?" he asked.

"That I can't say, but if these creatures came once there is no reason why they shouldn't come again. Certainly I gave them an uncomfortable time with the disintegrator gun, but by the next occasion they will be ready for it. Without going deeply into the matter, I should think they belong to another planet. I followed them into space, so it appears that the airless zero of the void has no terrors for them."

"Another planet?" Thorard repeated, puzzled. "Moyel, perhaps?"

Abna shrugged. "I don't think so. We never saw anything like this during our stay on the planet. I was thinking of the other two outer worlds in your system, which we've yet to examine. Anyway, let us pursue the analysis, then maybe we can tell you more."

The required facilities were immediately forthcoming, and Thorard returned to his work on the bomb, which he hoped would ultimately give the quartet the key to their own space. And, as the four worked on, examining every detail of the weird dead creature from space, the more astounded they became. At last Abna drew a deep breath and looked at the Amazon incredulously.

"Are you thinking what I'm thinking, Vi?" he asked.

"I'm thinking that this creature—and all the rest of

them—are nothing else but crystallized thought! Or, more correctly, they are the base products of mind reduced to the lower stratum of materiality. They are, in short, fragments of a diabolically evil mind reduced to material form."

"The Mind of Moyel!" Mexone exclaimed, snapping his fingers.

"That's it," the Amazon assented. "When we destroyed that machine housing the Mind, something must have happened. The Mind force imprisoned within the machine was dissipated into space. Radiations were instantly at work upon it and parts of it crystallized—I say 'crystallized' for want of a better term—and formed into units as evil as the original mind. Like can only produce like, so evil offspring from the original evil Mind could be the only answer. Evidently the entire mass of that exploded Mind didn't crystallize: only parts of it. Enough parts to number tens of thousands, all exhibiting the same baleful hate as the original Mind, but now in a material form."

"Then," Mexone said at length, "we're not really so much better off than we were before?"

"Yes, we are, to a certain extent," Abna answered. "We have not got the overpowering mental force of the Wave to fight, for one thing—and for another, these creatures are material so we can at least attack them. Their most deadly weapon is their hypnotic mental power, which must be pretty considerable when it is directly concentrated on one object."

"And how do you suppose Moyel is faring amidst

all this?" the Amazon asked. "Surely they must be suffering onslaught the same as the people here?"

"Possibly. There is only one thing to do. We must attack the creatures in the void and blast them to pieces."

CHAPTER ELEVEN
ROBOT ARMY

"I think," Abna said, after a thoughtful pause, "that there is only one complete solution to the difficulty, and it isn't altogether a guaranteed one. We must return to Moyel—the four of us that is—and use their mass production equipment for the creation of space-ships and robots. We can't do it fast enough here, but maybe we can there. There is, of course, the possibility that the creatures are as prevalent on Moyel as they are here, but there is better equipment there to deal with them. We'll wear our helmets so that we can be sure of no mental disturbance."

"But if the creatures are attacking us here, what good can you do on Moyel?" Thorard demanded.

"You will have to ring yourselves with defences as best you can until we can come back in such numbers as to be able to deal with them."

"And we continue our experiments with your bomb as formerly?"

"Certainly you do: that is essential. Now, we must waste no more time. Every second counts because these creatures are probably multiplying while we are waiting."

Abna did not spend any more time explaining. He hurried from the conference building with the Amazon, Viona, and Mexone following quickly after him. In a matter of a few minutes they were in the *Ultra* with the airlock closed. Abna settled himself at the control board, and within a few minutes the vessel was sweeping to the heights.

The journey through space to Moyel was quickly accomplished. The *Ultra* plunged into the midst of the hurtling clouds, was through them in an instant, and the familiar vision of Moyel's somber, dull landscape burst upon the vision. From their earlier readings of exact location of the underground laboratory, Abna was soon able to pinpoint that part of the nearby jungle wherein lay Marita's village. As the *Ultra* flew over the area at a low altitude, the Crusaders saw the mud huts but not a soul in sight.

"What's that?" Mexone asked abruptly, pointing.

The others gazed down fixedly, nor did it take them long to decide that what they were looking at was a sprawled figure, half buried in the loam and soft earth.

"Something definitely wrong," the Amazon said briefly. "Better descend, Abna, and we'll take a closer look."

Abna nodded and brought the machine down swiftly in the center of the compound. He wasted no time in opening the airlock, then he paused for a moment.

"Better put on your helmets. We've no idea what may happen, and it's better to be safe than sorry."

Helmets were duly buckled and weapons examined, then Abna led the way to the exterior, heading straight for the half-buried body that had been seen. He never reached it. There were so many other bodies on the way that he stopped at the first one he came to. It was not one of the Ajipurs, therefore it was presumably one of Marita's own race. There seemed to be considerable wounding about the face, as indeed was the case with the other bodies which Mexone, Viona, and the Amazon all came across. In fact, it was the Amazon who made the most significant discovery of all.

"Come and look," she said seriously, and one by one, Abna, Viona, and Mexone all identified the lacerated, dead face of little Marita, a look of stark terror in her eyes as she had died.

Abna clenched his fists and looked about him in the desolation.

"Only one answer to this, Vi," he said grimly. "Those infernal space creatures have struck here and killed everybody."

The Amazon nodded slowly. "That is the way it looks."

"I was fond of little Marita," Abna went on savagely. "I loved her almost as much as I do Viona. That she should be sacrificed to these filthy, evil things...." He stopped, at a loss for words for the moment so intense was his fury.

"We'll avenge her, Abna," the Amazon said deliberately, "even if it takes us the rest of our lives. Meanwhile, it looks as if all chance of civilization being restored has been ended."

"One advantage," Mexone pointed out. "If the creatures tried to attack the machinery, which they probably did, it is of too tough a constitution to be harmed. From what we saw, coming down, it was all in order. We'd better go and have a look."

"The rest of you go with Mexone," Abna said. "I'll follow you—after I've buried little Marita."

* * * * * * *

As the Crusaders had expected, the laboratory machinery—which now lay exposed in a gigantic hollow—was still intact.

"Might as well get busy right away," Abna said. "There don't seem to be any storms brewing at the moment, so it's a good chance. You can help me, Vi. You two—" he glanced at Mexone and Viona—"had better stay on constant watch in case the creatures attack. If they do, use the *Ultra*'s weapons and give us good warning to take cover."

They nodded and promptly returned to the *Ultra*, leaving Abna and the Amazon to issue their orders to the mathematical machine, which, in turn, would transmit them to the slave machines. This was not a task that took very long, the details being fresh in the minds of the pair—and also this time there was no Mind present to start any trouble.

In a matter of thirty minutes the first two robots were complete, and standing ready for orders, while others were in the process of rapid manufacture.

Days and nights passed on the crazy, storm-blasted world of Moyel while the work continued apace. There was some difficulty at first in teaching the robots how to control the space machines, but eventually their mechanical brains seemed capable of taking it in and they responded magnificently. Within a fortnight nearly fifty of the machines were in the air, undergoing test, piloted without flaw, and by 'beings' that could not know either fear or death.

"I fancy," Abna said, surveying the busy scene of activity, "that our bird-like invaders are in for a shock when they next attack. In some ways I wish they'd hurry up about it. It would give these robots of ours some practice under actual battle conditions."

The very next day his wish was gratified. Suddenly, as though the creatures had suddenly realized that they still had enemies left on Moyel, an invasion broke upon the planet. Nothing that had happened on Falsen could even compare with it; it gave the quartet some idea of how many of the things there really were.

From north, south, east, and west they came, a solid driving cloud, so thick in formation it was impossible to glimpse the gray sky between their ranks. They were evidently directed by some kind of leader, for they did not even hesitate in finding their objective. They drove with all their strength and venom straight to the ranks of the robots while another detachment headed for the human quartet. In this latter enterprise there was failure, however. The Amazon, Abna, Viona, and Mexone had already seen what was coming and promptly escaped into the shelter of the *Ultra*. Once inside it, with the airlock shut, they hurried to the huge observation window and watched events.

Very intriguing events they were, too. At least fifty of the creatures dashed themselves to death against the window; so tremendous was their velocity and so transparent the window, they had imagined they had a clear field. Others realized what was happening, swung aside, sprayed the observation window with deadly venom, and veered off in search of easier prey.

Not that the robots were easy to tackle: far from it. They knew only blind obedience to the orders they had received, and they followed the orders out to the letter. Some managed to get space machines into the air and wreaked death and havoc on all sides amidst the whizzing hordes. Those left on the ground attacked the creatures with their pincer hands and literally tore the creatures in pieces whenever they had the chance. Nor did the creatures' hypnotic powers have any effect on the robots. The orders of the humans were indelibly engraved on the electronic brains, and no other orders, hypnotic or otherwise, could supersede them.

In the end the hordes realized they had taken on more than they could tackle. They began to retreat.

All eyes were fixed on the hordes as at last the last one departed from Moyel. Thereafter the great army of them fled onwards into space, dark and menacing against the further stars. When at length there was a reasonable distance between them, Abna started the *Ultra* moving forward again steadily, and he continued to maintain the intervening distance until the creatures were obviously slowing down and congregating in one enormous mass.

"Just look at them!" Viona exclaimed breathlessly. "Just hovering there in space, without air, and in the midst of the most unthinkable conditions.... Dad, how can anything live unconcerned with no air and a temperature of absolute zero?"

"Don't ask me, Viona! Our type of life isn't suited to that, but it's obviously normal to these things. So that's where they congregate, is it? Must be a million of them there at least.... Mark their position by the stars behind them, then we'll know next time."

This was duly done, and with extreme care—then the return journey to Moyel began.

And back on that planet, at the end of a fortnight the army of robots and spaceships had trebled its original size. At the end of a month, storms not withstanding, the whole area that had formerly been covered by the laboratory was a mass of spaceships from end to end, and every hour they were increasing. Robots themselves were legion, still performing their particular tasks until instructed to do otherwise.

"Time we called a halt," Abna decided, surveying. "We've got all we want now. Nothing else left but to launch the attack. Incidentally, I suppose you've noticed that there have been no onslaughts by the creatures since the last belting they got?"

"True enough," the Amazon admitted. "They evidently learned their lesson. I'm just wondering if they vented their spite on Falsen instead. Might contact them by radio and find out."

Viona crossed to the radio, and in another moment contact had been established. After some delay the voice of Thorard came through.

"Greetings, my friends! It's a pleasure to hear from you after so long an interval. I trust all goes well with you?"

"Everything's perfect," Abna answered, taking the microphone from Viona. "We've located the hideout of the creatures, and have now prepared an army big enough to smash them. Have they invaded your world at all while we've been away?"

"Several times," Thorard answered gloomily. "With the same disastrous results. Several hundreds of our people have been killed. The attacks seem to be in greater numbers and with greater violence each time."

"That is coming to an end," Abna declared. "We are setting off almost immediately to launch an attack of our own, and we have every reason to believe that it will be successful.... Of even more vital interest is the bomb I asked you to construct. How are you progressing?"

"Very well indeed. We have been constructing two bombs, and have completed the main details. Anytime now we shall have a test bomb complete. We intend to fire the test bomb into space and study its reactions, before finalizing the remaining bomb for use by yourselves."

"Into space?" Abna repeated.

"We are using one of the small space machines which you have shown us how to build. Naturally, we cannot fire a bomb like that anywhere on our planet in order to test it: it is too violent. Space is the obvious answer. The moment we have results we'll transmit them to you. Indeed, by that time, you may possibly have returned here?"

"Let us hope so," Abna responded. "Farewell for the time being, Thorard. We'll see what we can do."

Abna cut the contact and turned. Since the others had heard everything he had no need of comment. The Amazon crossed to the control board and depressed the switch that livened the external loudspeaker. She spoke with the sharp incisiveness necessary to implant orders in the electronic brains of the robots.

"Here are your instructions. Cease construction work at once and prepare to attack. You know exactly what to do from your earlier training. You will follow this giant machine and go into action when we do."

Abna crossed to the control board and waited with his hand on the power switch. By the window, the Amazon, Viona, and Mexone stood watching the hordes of robots on the move, each following a predetermined plan and entering the particular spaceship assigned to it.

"Right!" the Amazon announced at length. "They're all in their required places. We can start."

The power switch moved under Abna's hand. With effortless ease the *Ultra* began to rise, swept over the multitude of spaceships containing the robots, and thereafter continued on its way to the upper heights of the atmosphere. The Amazon kept a constant watch and presently nodded in satisfaction.

"They're following, Abna—just as we told them to."

Indeed they were, a tremendous armada of small and deadly machines—quite the biggest spatial army that had ever lifted from Moyel. They moved steadily, in perfect formation, guided and controlled by beings who could not make a mistake and to whom fear was an unknown quantity.

"We shouldn't be so far away from them now," Viona said presently. "The stars check with our line of flight."

Abna promptly slowed down and peered intently into the velvet blackness of the void. At first he saw only the stars, then after a moment or two he became aware of some of them being transiently blotted out as something intervened between him and them. The longer he stared, and the nearer the *Ultra* came, the more it became evident that there was something in space—a vast area of darkest gray. Against anything else the intervening mass would have been blackest-black, but there was nothing that could ever approach the awful dark of outer space. Everything else was muddy by comparison.

"They're there, the whole demon's horde of them," Abna said grimly. "What do you suggest? Searchlight them and then sweep in to the attack?"

"Best thing," the Amazon agreed; and turned to the space radio again. "Attention!" she called. "These are your new orders, countermanding all others. You will switch on your searchlights, aiming them in the direction of this leader machine. You will keep them on until instructed otherwise, the aim being to so blind and confuse the enemy that they will not be able to retaliate. Release your weapons when I give the final order. Communication ends."

"That should do it," Abna nodded. "Viona, Mexone— take over the weapons. Vi, you stand by the window to give the final order to the robots, then also take a weapon yourself when you've done that. Okay?"

"Okay," the Amazon agreed.

Abna waited a moment or two for the necessary positions to be taken up, kept his hand on the power switch ready for immediate action—then with his other hand he snapped on the searchlight.

It blasted a blinding blue-white beam of brilliance into the void, illuminating an immense section of the mind-creatures. They were apparently at rest, hundreds of thousands of them, hanging motionless in the void and evidently sustained by the invisible but—to them—revitalizing properties of spatial radiation. At the touch of the glaring brilliance they stirred somewhat—only to be met by a battery of lights as all the other searchlights came into being as well.

"Right—let them have it!" The Amazon's eyes were glinting with the light of battle as she swung to the window. "And while we blast them to powder, let us remember the hapless peoples of Falsen and Moyel, and particularly poor, inoffensive Marita. Kill them! Destroy them!"

From right, left, center, top, and bottom poured the tide of destruction. The creatures could not possibly escape from it. Fifteen minutes perhaps—no more, and the void was free of the blight. Not a single creature remained. The only traces were in cosmic dust drifting on the ceaseless currents of spatial radiation.

The Amazon switched off her proton gun with a satisfied sigh and then slid from the saddle. Viona and Mexone did likewise. They turned to find Abna grinning.

"That seems to have taken care of that," he commented. "In that particular field our work is now done. Two planets released from trouble. The rest's up to Thorard. Better have a word with him."

The Amazon switched on the radio and intoned deliberately. After a moment or two Thorard's voiee responded.

"All's well, Thorard," the Amazon announced. "Every one of the creatures has been destroyed, so you've nothing further to worry about on that score."

"That is wonderful news indeed. I do congratulate and thank you from the bottom of my heart."

Abna signaled and the Amazon retired from the microphone.

"There's a whole planet here, Thorard, for the taking over," Abna said. "All you need are the necessary spaceships and crews, plus your scientific knowledge, and the job's done."

"Splendid!" Thorard exclaimed. "I will put the necessary plans in hand for planetary development right away. First we have the bomb to test."

"How far on are you?" Abna questioned. "That is our only interest now—getting back into our own space."

"Final tests are being made. We should have a result at any time. Come back to Falsen, then we can give you the details."

"We'll be back in no time," Abna promised. "Along with an army of space machines and robots, which you can use for the colonization of Moyel. 'Bye for now."

He switched off and turned back to the controls.

"Looks as though we're going to return in state," the Amazon commented. "If not that, then with our retinue." Bethinking herself, she switched on the space radio. "Attention leader!" she called. "Proceed to planet directly ahead—Falsen by name. Alight there and await further orders, either from me or from whoever shall be in control. Orders from one named Thorard will be quite legitimate. Message ends."

She switched off again and watched the swarm proceeding ahead, moving with greater swiftness than the *Ultra*, because their lesser size made them able to pick up speed more rapidly in the shorter term.

"Quite a useful army for Thorard to use in colonization," the Amazon mused. "Ready-made for—"

She broke off, suddenly alerting. Her abrupt silence was so unexpected that the others looked at her in surprise. She was standing at the window, completely tensed, her eyes fixed on something in the void. It—whatever it was—was between the retreating robot machines and the *Ultra*, occupying a clear stretch of void. Mexone moved across to look, and then Viona. They were completely puzzled by what they saw.

Something, like a purple dot, was forming in space. In a few seconds it grew larger, like a gigantic amethyst. Its transition to this new shape was like a gentle merging, like colors flowing together to form an absolute dark mauve.

"What the—" Mexone exclaimed, puzzled—then suddenly Viona let out a cry.

"It's a bomb! A repetition of the bomb that hurled us into this space—"

"You're right!" the Amazon agreed sharply. "It's working a bit more slowly than the previous bombs, perhaps because of the chemistry and mathematics being different, but we—"

"Thorard and his fellow scientists must have fired it into space," Abna said quickly, gazing through his own observation window. "They did say they were going to— Have to detour sharply."

He swung the controls of the *Ultra* and the huge vessel responded immediately, but at that instant something happened. The increasing ball of purple outside suddenly exploded, and with a staggering violence. First there came a flash that seemed to illuminate the universe, and with it the quartet in the *Ultra* blinked their eyes savagely to make certain they had not been blinded. Through a seeming haze of orange and red they beheld the purple ball mysteriously shrinking, not expanding into infinity, as had been the case on the previous two occasions. Following the initial flash, the core of the phenomenon was closing in on itself, like an exploding bomb photographed backwards.

"It's implosion!" Abna cried, jumping up. "Not explosion. The very thing we asked Thorard for. The bomb's imploding inwardly and we—"

He had no chance to say any more as the bomb's effects suddenly caught up with them. The *Ultra*, huge though it was, was gripped suddenly in an invisible vortex and drawn sideways from the course it had been following. Abna made a frantic effort to restore things with the controls but it was a hopeless task. The bomb's mystic powers were irresistible. The quartet, flung to the floor, felt as if they were in a gigantic vice.

The robot fleet was just clear of the implosion, and sailed on its way, the robots themselves mechanically oblivious to the disappearance of the *Ultra*. They had received their orders and that was enough. They would continue on their way until Falsen was reached.

And the *Ultra*? Gradually the four within felt their senses returning to them as that overwhelming pressure relaxed from their lungs and hearts. They stirred on the floor, and little by little managed to get to their feet and look outside. They saw what seemed to be a huge semi-circle which sheared off vaguely at the base as though in another dimension. Inside it, appeared countless pinpricks of light and on the outside edge, blazing points of light. It dominated everything.

"Where in cosmos are we?" the Amazon demanded at last; and after a long spell of thought Abna answered her.

"Half in one space and half in another. That's my guess."

"Half in—" Viona began, turning. "But how do you mean?"

"Believe it or not, I think the bomb experiment has been only half-successful—or rather partly successful. We've been sucked inwards by the implosion of the core, but the bomb has not been quite powerful enough to complete the job. That semi-circle we see there is, I'm convinced, the Universe from which we came."

The Amazon, Viona, and Mexone stared at it.

"That—the Universe?" the Amazon exclaimed.

"We know the Universe is circular, one molecule in a macro-universe. That is what we are seeing now, with the lower half of the perfect circle veered off because we're half in one universe and half in another. Beyond the perimeter we see the giant universe in which we have been having our experiences. Don't forget we are of gigantic size: that's why we see our normal Universe as a semi-circle, because we are not attuned to it."

"How do we get out?" the Amazon asked at length, a touch of consternation in her voice. "Hovering between the two, we're worse off than we were before."

Abna smiled. "Having got this far, Vi, we'll finish it! The answer is not in physical movement, but in reduction in size. As we reduce size we'll obviously become too small for the larger Universe to hold us any longer. We'll assimilate with the smaller one—our own. And that is what we have to do."

"Not very easy, is it?" the Amazon asked, shrugging. "We've got everything aboard this *Ultra* except machinery for reducing size. It's the one thing we didn't think of, perhaps because we didn't foresee such a thing being necessary."

"We haven't got the apparatus," Abna admitted, "but at least we've got machine-tool equipment and tons of spare material for any use whatever. On top of that, we've got computers to check our figures."

"You mean make the necessary machinery?" The Amazon looked thoughtful for a moment. "Have you forgotten that mathematics are different here? It won't be easy."

"We'll work on the basis of two and two making five instead of the four to which we are accustomed. The computers will respond from that basis. We'll cut out all our own ideas on mathematics and let the machines do it for us. And the sooner the better."

Abna turned to the instruments and spent several minutes working out the basic equations on the modification that the multiple of two by two equaled five. This done he fed the first of the figures into the No. 1 machine, got the answer, and then proceeded to No. 2. So, little by little, he and the Amazon between them waded through the complications of the basic mathematics and left the machines to provide the answers. An involved and highly technical formula began to build up—the formula for the reduction of electronic orbits to the point of zero, the only applicable number to signify diminishment into the absolute.

In all, this supreme effort took several hours, but

at the end of it there were the necessary details all complete, together with the figurative specifications for the equipment required to produce such a shrinkage.

"Right! So far so good!" Abna exclaimed in satisfaction, surveying the reports. "Our job now is to sketch designs for the instruments and then have the machine-tool apparatus turn them into actual fact."

The work went on ceaselessly, hour after hour, and outside the incredible view of the Earth-universe remained stationary—as indeed did the *Ultra*. No movement was needed or called for, for the present position between spaces was ideal, and anyway the figuring had all been calculated from that basis.

The quartet worked in relays. They rested, they worked, they ate. Occasionally, even, they slept, but most of the time they relied on restorative tablets to keep them alert. Nothing mattered anymore except a return to their own Universe and the things they could understand.

So, finally, the job was done. The Reducer—as they had named it—stood in the central passageway, linked up to the power plant and supplied with all the needful controls. In itself the apparatus looked simple enough: it was in the profound internal workings where the secret lay.

"Everything seems to be in order," Abna said, giving it a last inspection. "A triumph over the peculiar mathematics of the macro-universe. Are you ready to sample it?"

"Of course," the Amazon responded. "It surely

can't produce any effects more painful than we've had already. Let it go."

She crossed to the window and stood waiting. Viona and Mexone joined her. They heard Abna's hand snapping the switches, and there followed a deep, all-pervading whine.

It was a slow, unhurried process as the mathematics of the Reducer became more and more complicated, handling the increasing complexities of the situation with flawless smoothness. The energy also radiating from the machine, by which the electronic orbits were reduced, also radiated with never a second's interruption, calling upon the inexhaustible supply of copper within the power plant.

Silent and fascinated, the four watched this wondrous and fantastic return from the Universe of giantism to the Universe of normalcy. They saw the perimeter of the semi-circle expand constantly until it had swallowed up the outer stars, until it was the only thing in existence and the supra-universe beyond had gone. Still the electronic shrinkage continued until the swarms of closely spaced dots of light had widened out into normal stellar distances.

Abna turned slowly to the control board, then paused for a moment with a look of surprise.

"Incidentally, where are we going? Not back to Earth surely? Among these tens of thousands of worlds, many populated—not always by a form of life that we can understand, but life just the same—there must be others who need our help. So, where do we go next?"

"That's a queer-looking star," Viona said at last—and she nodded towards one solitary point standing a little apart from its neighbors. Actually the distance from the nearest neighbor was huge, but from their vantage point it only seemed a mere hop.

"It's not a star: it's a planet," the Amazon said. "The disc is plain. If it were a star that would not be so... gleaming like silver. I never saw a world7 so intensely bright, considering there is no sun anywhere near it. And yet it does not look like an internal brightness either."

Abna looked, too.

"That," he said slowly, "is a world which somehow radiates happiness! I can sense it, yet I do not know why it should...."

"No harm in finding out," Viona said, her eyes bright with eagerness.

Abna nodded and said nothing. He activated the ship's mighty engines and the *Ultra* began to sweep silently into the void, toward that glowing world whose attraction grew with every passing second.

ABOUT THE AUTHOR

British writer JOHN RUSSELL FEARN was born near Manchester, England, in 1908. As a child he devoured the science fiction of Wells and Verne, and was a voracious reader of the Boys' Story Papers. He was also fascinated by the cinema, and first broke into print in 1931 with a series of articles in *Film Weekly*.

He then quickly sold his first novel, *The Intelligence Gigantic*, to the American magazine, *Amazing Stories*. Over the next fifteen years, writing under several pseudonyms, Fearn became one of the most prolific contributors to all of the leading US science fiction pulps, including such legendary publications as *Astounding Stories*, *Startling Stories*, *Thrilling Wonder Stories*, and *Weird Tales*.

During the late 1940s he diversified into writing novels for the UK market, and also created his famous superwoman character, The Golden Amazon, for the prestigious Canadian magazine, the Toronto *Star Weekly*. In the early 1950s in the UK, his fifty-two novels as "Vargo Statten" were bestsellers, most notably his novelization of the film, *Creature from the Black Lagoon*.

Apart from science fiction, he had equal success with westerns, romances, and detective fiction, writing an amazing total of 180 novels—most of them in a period of just ten years—before his early death in 1960. His work has been translated into nine languages, and continues to be reprinted and read worldwide.